WOODHAVEN

L.J. DOUGHERTY

This book is a work of fiction.

First Edition Paperback
No part of this publication may be reproduced or transmitted in any form without written permission from the author. All rights reserved.

ISBN: 979-8-9863191-0-0

For Tia.
Thank you for always loving my dark and brooding side.

1

———————

Dad's grip never loosens from around my hand. He pulls me along with him, the way we used to cross intersections when I was a toddler.

The sirens blare, warning of some impending disaster about to befall the city they're booming from. Screams of anger and pain escape and find us between the gaps. And then the gunfire begins.

"Dig," Dad says, and hands me a shovel. I look back at our vehicle parked on the shoulder of the dirt road, trunk still popped. "Come on, Joy."

He shovels scoop after scoop of dirt over his shoulder, burrowing down beside the patch of sunflower stalks.

"Dad?"

"Come on, Joy. We gotta move fast. Help me dig."

And I do.

The sounds in the distance continue. Sirens. And gunfire. And muffled voices shouting through bullhorns.

Dad and I dig until we are standing in a hole four feet deep, and that's when the tip of my shovel hits something other than soil. Dad drops to his knees, his fingers finding the edges of a metal crate, which he dusts off and pops open, revealing three handguns, three canteens and a duffle bag.

Seconds later, Dad has me by the hand again, guiding me back across the field to our car. He tosses the shovels into the trunk, beside the gas canisters, and we're back on the road. The glow of the city out my window is... I don't know what it is... Terrifying.

It isn't until Dad touches my arm that I realized my whole body is shaking. In the movies, this would be the point where the father tells his daughter that everything is going to be okay. But Dad doesn't say that. He doesn't lie.

We drive for hours, never once getting onto the freeway. The beams of our headlights reveal blowing dust and nothing else.

Dad clicks on the radio, but the words are just random gibberish by the time they make it through the fog of my mind.

... Mass arrests...

... Liberty...

... are no longer in control.

... what we've been waiting for since...

... lining people up against...

God.

Bless.

America.

I want to say something. About Mom. But it isn't the time.

"We need to stay focused," Dad had told me when he dragged me out of our home. "We need to get out of the city."

He said that roadblocks would go up soon, and if we got stopped by the wrong people, I needed to be ready to use my gun. He explained we may get lucky and get to where we're headed before the powers that be can organize enough to lock everything down. I didn't have to ask him how he knew all of this. It was clear it's what he'd been preparing me for.

The buzz of his cellphone rattles the cup holder. He scoops it up and answers. "Where are you?"

Freddy's voice replies over speaker, "Just got off I-81. Shit's piling up."

"I told you to take Tungsten."

"I-81's usually faster."

"Ain't no more usually, Freddy. You still have the address?"

"Yeah. Written down right here."

"Memorize it and eat it."

"I'm not gonna—"

"I said, eat it, goddamnit! You think I'm fuckin' around?"

There's silence from Freddy's end of the line.

"And smash your phone after this. Hope we see you at the cabin."

Dad ends the call and hands me his phone. "Take out the card. Same with yours."

"What if we need to call someone for help?" I ask.

"There's no one able to help us now, Joy."

He makes me snap the SIM cards in half and toss everything out the window. As the dirt swallows them up behind us, a tether I didn't know existed is severed.

2

I can still hear the faint sound of emergency sirens in the distance as we press on through the deep snow, shoving mounds of it out of our path through the thin aspens. Dad's duffle bag is heavier than mine, nearly filled to the brim with the day's finds. I keep my rifle slung across my chest, just like him, and we make our way up a steep incline leading to the icy road.

Dad quietly pulls himself up onto the shoulder, the snow crunching beneath his body as he readies his rifle. Reaching down with his free hand, he pulls me up. That's when I see what he can't stop staring at. Two cars wedged together in a heap of twisted metal, the aftermath of a head-on collision, smoke still billowing lightly from the crumpled engines. The closest vehicle is a black Cadillac, like something I've seen in a government motorcade. The other, a basic green junker.

Dad walks slowly toward the wreckage, stopping at the Cadillac. Even from the shoulder I can see the driver, his face pulverized against the bent steering wheel. I wait at a distance, keeping watch in both directions for visitors.

"Dad?" I whisper. He ignores me, trying to open the back door of the Cadillac. It's bent shut. He reaches in through the broken window and I'm unable to see what he's straining for. "Dad." My voice is still hushed.

He pulls a metal briefcase out through the window, dragging something along with it—something it takes my mind a moment to comprehend. A man's arm, attached at the wrist by a shiny pair of handcuffs. Blood runs down the palm and fingers, coming out from beneath the sleeve of the suit jacket.

"Bring me your knife," Dad says.

"What?" I'm not sure why I say it. I heard him clearly. Maybe it was just a way to delay what I know is coming.

"Your knife," he repeats. I unsheathe the bowie from my hip strap and cross the road. It's slick, only a thin layer of powder covering the sheet of ice layered over the asphalt. Stopping by his side, I can see the other two men in the Cadillac, both wearing dark suits, both lying lifelessly in the back seat.

I hand Dad the giant blade and he immediately starts slicing into the dead man's wrist, just above the handcuff.

"Dad?" He ignores me again and I watch, disgusted, but at the same time forcing myself to stomach it. The severed hand falls into the snow and the briefcase is free. Dad sets it on the trunk of the Cadillac and pauses. I'm about to ask—then I see the keyhole.

"Check their pockets," he says, motioning inside the vehicle. Looking through the window at the dead passengers, I want to plead with him not to make me. I want to drop to my knees next to the disembodied hand and beg him. But I'm the smaller of the two of us, and more nimble. This was where I pull my weight.

"Climb in there and check." I hesitate, glancing at Dad, but he just stares back at me, waiting for me to do as I'm told.

I hate myself for it, but I begin to cry.

His heavy hands settle on my shoulders and he tells me, "Hey. Hey. It's gonna be alright now. Just—we gotta take what we can. You know? We still got a ways to go till we reach the cabin and every little bit helps." He uses his index finger to raise my chin so our eyes meet. It was the gentlest I'd seen him since it all went down.

Taking a deep breath, I compose myself and climb in through the broken window. I slide across the first dead body—the one missing his hand—and sit down in the middle seat. Pulling his suit jacket open, I see a 9mm strapped into a leather shoulder holster beneath the armpit. I remove it and stuff it inside my coat, then continue searching the pockets.

Nothing.

On to the next corpse. This one's head is stuck between the driver's seat and the driver's door. His neck must have compacted on impact. It's all grey and purply looking. I scour through all of his pockets one at a time. He too is armed with a 9mm—but no key. I grab his gun and look out the window at Dad.

"The driver," he says.

I reach around from the back seat, grab hold of the shoulders, and pull. At first he won't budge, his face wrapped around the top of the steering wheel as though his forehead was trying to eat it. It reminds me of that photo of the big oak tree that grew around the tricycle, swallowing the back half.

After a few more tugs, the face finally releases its grip, oozing with blood as the demolished skull peels away. What's left of the head sloshes back against the headrest, and I try to balance him upright. Reaching into his breast pocket, I feel it. Dad sees my eyes widen and I hold it up into view.

A small electronic key.

He helps me back out of the car, and I give it to him. He swallows hard, inserts it, and pops open the briefcase. Stacks of hundred-dollar bills fill the inside. Disappointed, he sighs and dumps the cash out onto the ice, then tosses the case aside.

The junker is next. He leans in through the broken window and comes back out with a tattered backpack. It looks like the kind an elementary school aged kid would carry, colorful with a cartoon platypus on it. Dad unzips it, revealing an assortment of canned food. He shows me. "This."

My legs feel numb and I sit down on the road. I can't think straight. Mentally exhausted. Dad bends down and puts his arms around me. "I'm here for you, baby. We're here for each other. No matter what happens."

And sixteen months pass.

3

———

As my eyes open, I'm unsure whether the knock was part of my dream, but when the second series of taps rattle the front door, a surge of adrenaline replaces my grogginess. I hear Dad moving steadily down the hallway from his room, past mine, to the staircase, the steps moaning as he descends. I slide from my bed and crack my door enough to see down to the first floor where Dad stands, the double-barrel shotgun seated on his shoulder. He presses his ear gently against the front door of the cabin.

Another knock. He backs away and aims the shotgun. "Who is it?"

From the other side of the door, I hear a muffled voice respond. "It's Freddy."

My tension eases a bit. He made it back from his trip of the mountain.

Dad cocks the shotgun. "Where the hell you been?"

"You gonna let me in? It's fucking freezing out here!"

Dad hesitates, then lowers the shotgun and opens the door. Freddy stands in the doorway, and even through the unkempt, bushy beard, I can make out the defeated expression on his face.

"Sorry," Freddy says as a pistol comes out of the darkness, pressing against the side of his head. A stranger steps into view, his steady hand gripping the weapon.

Dad whips the shotgun back up.

Oh, God. Oh, God.

"Let's step inside. Shall we?" The man's voice sounds funny. Definitely from a different part of the country. He's standing just beyond the glow coming from the candles burning inside the cabin, making it difficult to see his features.

"No," Dad responds with his usual level of confidence. "I think we're all good where we're at."

Freddy, the human shield, is trembling.

"In that case, I'll rephrase," the stranger says. "Drop the double barrel and back up."

Dad doesn't waver. "Who the hell is this, Freddy?"

"This is Roger," Freddy says, the man's pistol still pressed into his temple.

"I'm Roger," the man confirms. "And I'm coming inside."

Freddy gives Dad a slight nod, like he's trying to assure him everything will be better if he does what he's told. Dad doesn't listen to Freddy's advice very often. He's smarter than Freddy. And both of them know it. But the pleading expression on Freddy's face is eating at him. He backs up slowly and leans the shotgun against our handmade wooden table that we'd eaten at in silence just a few hours prior.

The stranger—Roger—ushers Freddy inside and gently closes the door behind him with his heel. Keeping the gun against Freddy's head, he unslings a leather satchel from his shoulder and tosses it aside. It lands with substantial weight against the floorboards.

They're all closer to the candles now and I can see the bruises on Freddy's face. I know Dad sees them too.

"He do that?" Dad asks.

Freddy's about to answer when Roger cuts him off. "Have a seat, Warren."

How's he know Dad's name?

Dad sits at the table, eyeing Roger aggressively. I've seen Dad look at men like this before, but it's been a long time. Of course, it's been a long time since we've seen anyone at all other than Freddy.

There's a collective aura of surprise when Roger finally lowers the pistol. "Go on and make us some tea, Freddy." His voice is even, his demeanor calm.

"Tea?" Freddy asks.

"You have tea, Warren?" Roger inquires.

"Yeah," Dad gestures to the stove.

"Then yes, tea."

Freddy doesn't need any more direction. He grabs the kettle, fills it at the sink, and pulls down some loose-leaf from the cabinet. Roger takes a seat at the table across from Dad and they stare at one another for a moment in silence.

"Well?" Dad says. "What do you want from us?"

"Safety."

"Don't we all?" Dad glances over at Freddy, who stands idly by at the stove. "You two known each other long?"

Freddy fidgets. "Picked me up a few days back."

Dad nods at the pistol in Roger's hand. "Picked you up?"

"Freddy says you've been up here for quite some time now. Says you knew everything was going to happen the way it did."

Dad's focus drifts back to Roger. "I had a feelin'. Was just a matter of time."

"And all this," Roger says, looking around the cabin. "You had this all prepared?" Dad just stares at him. "Impressive."

"Not what people used to say," Dad admits. And he taps his middle and index fingers three times on the tabletop. It's his signal. It's my cue.

"Yeah. Guess you might have looked a little crazy back then, huh? Freddy filled me in."

"What else did Freddy fill you in on?"

Roger casually points his pistol at Warren's chest. "He told me you had a daughter. And my assumption would be that she's the one crouched up on those stairs with the rifle pointed at me."

I stare down the sights of my .30-06. I'm aiming it at his face. His eyes clock me.

"That'd be her."

I'm prone on one knee, my finger resting on the trigger. Dad taught me to only touch it if my intention is to pull it, and right now, if things go sour, my intention is to do just that.

The tea kettle whistles.

"It would be in your best interest to instruct her to put it down."

"I think it would be in your best interest to leave my home," Dad says. Freddy is entirely focused on the standoff, oblivious to the whistling kettle beside him.

Roger looks up at me, his pistol still aimed at Dad's chest. "What's your name, my dear?" I don't respond. Then, in a voice so casual it sounds like he's about to fall asleep, he says, "Take the damn teapot off the stove, for Christ's sake, Freddy." It's enough to snap him out of it and he lifts the kettle off the burner. The whistling fades out into silence. "You asked who I was. I'm a desperate man in search of safety, and the only way to guarantee safety is to take it from someone more prepared than I."

"There ain't no guarantees no more. Especially not when it comes to stayin' safe. Point proven in our current situation," Dad says.

Roger turns to Freddy. "Are you gonna pour us a cup?" Freddy breathes in more than I think his lungs can hold. He's seeing how this is all going to play out. He's seeing what I see. But he pours the tea anyway, his hands shaking the entire time.

Roger raises the cup and enjoys the scent, his other hand still gripping the pistol, still pointing it at Dad. He says to me, "How long can you hold that thing?" I keep my aim. He grins. "Alright then." And he sets the cup back down to cool. No one else touches their tea.

"What's your plan?" Dad asks him. "Surely you had one before walking through my front door."

"I'd like to stay here for a while. Keep my head covered. Keep out of the searchlight. Now, I knew that because of the way things are nowadays, there was no way you'd let some stranger into your home by choice. It's just too risky. Too dangerous. Can't take chances like that anymore. People out there, they're not much better than rabid animals. Sooner kill you than shake your hand. But I'm not like them, and from what Freddy here tells me, neither are you. So I'd like to propose something. You allow me to stay here—and rest assured I will be staying here, though I'd prefer to have your blessing—you let me stay, and I'll help you protect this place. I'll make it my one and only objective to keep the four of us from befalling any harm from those people out there."

Dad is skeptical. "And how will you do that?" He takes a drink. "With that little pistol?"

"With everything I've got."

"You ain't got nothin' else."

"Though your daughter and you may be well versed in firearms and survival skills, two individuals cannot fortify this cabin. Hell, I got in right away. There's strength in numbers. You lose balance when you add too many folks to the equation, but keep it at the right size and there's nothing we can't defend against."

Dad shakes his head, his finger and thumb tightening around the small ceramic handle of the cup. "We ain't gotta defend against nothin'. Ain't no one lookin' for us up here. Ain't no one comin' 'round. Only reason you found us is you pried our existence outta Freddy."

Freddy perks up and says, "Warren, I think it might be a good idea to—"

"This here's my home. Me and my daughter, that's who it's for." I can hear the anger swelling in Dad's voice as he tries to stay cool. "Like you said yourself, I'm not lettin' some stranger stay here. You can't keep that gun on me forever. So you can either take your chance at shootin' us both down right now, or you can walk out that door."

Roger and Dad stare one another down like a pair of gunslingers. I can't help but think of that scene in Barry Lyndon, the duel with Captain Quin. Dad may not be holding a weapon, but from the way he's facing the armed intruder, you'd think he must be.

Freddy stands by.

"Doesn't have to be that way, Warren."

"It does," Dad says.

"I'm not going back out into those woods. Not going back out into that world. All it's become, I need to shut out. The situation's simple. You'd like to keep your daughter safe, keep your home safe? Letting me stay here is the way to make that happen. We can start firing off shots and realistically at the end of it all it'll be Freddy and your daughter cleaning up the mess—or you can make the choice right now to be a good person, a kind person, and an overly generous host, and simply allow me to shack up with you and yours."

Dad is silent as Roger leans in closer to him across the table and continues, "Are you like all those other brutal, selfish sons of bitches out there? Or are you still a good person?"

"Asks the man with his finger on the trigger."

Roger grins again, un-cocks the pistol and sets in down on the table. "You're right."

Freddy looks up at me, expecting to see me lower my rifle in response —but I'm not ready to lower my rifle. Not yet. Not till Dad gives me the signal.

Roger is smiling widely and says, "So, then—"

Without a seconds hesitation Dad slaps the pistol off the table, grabs his shotgun by the barrel and swings it viciously at Roger. The stock smashes against his head, sending the stranger to the floor.

4

———————

It's raining.

Roger's eyes peel open as he regains consciousness. It takes him a moment to realize he's been bound to one of the kitchen chairs with black electrical tape. We used an entire roll.

I sit across the room from him, my rifle across my lap, and we stare at one another. It was probably Dad's voice that woke him, coming from his bedroom on the second floor. Roger's gaze drifts. From where he's sitting, he can see straight up the stairs.

"One reason. Give me one damned reason I should," we hear Dad say.

"I owe him," Freddy answers. I can hear the floorboards croaking as the two of them pace about beyond the door. "He saved my life, Warren."

"So you say."

"He's not a bad guy."

"He forced his way into my home with a gun."

"You would have shot him on sight if he hadn't. Just because he's not an idiot doesn't make him dangerous."

"That's exactly what it makes him!"

Roger's sights move back to me and my rifle. "Your father seems quite adamant," he says.

"He's quick to decide," I respond with as much confidence as I can muster. It's the first time he hears my voice and I can see his body react subtly.

"Good trait to have. Sometimes." He pauses a moment. "Do you like it up here? All things considered?" I look down at my rifle and my fingers trace the polished wood grain of the stock. When he realizes that I'm not going to answer, he continues. "How long have you been here?"

"What's it to you?" I ask.

"I'm a people person. I enjoy hearing backstories."

I look him in the eye and say, "You first, then."

"What would you like to know?"

"Where were you when everything happened?"

"I was at work."

"Where did you work?"

"I was a teacher."

He doesn't look like any of the teachers from my old school. They were all old or overweight. This guy is... "What subject?"

"History."

"What grade?"

Roger smiles. "Seventh." This makes me pause. If I were still in school, that's the grade I'd be in next year. Maybe I would have even been in his class. I think to ask him what school he worked at, but decide it doesn't matter.

"Are you married?"

"No."

He's handsome. At least I think he would be if times were like before. If he got a shower, a shave and a fresh set of clothes. Maybe two showers. "Why not?" I ask.

He doesn't answer that one. "Where were *you*?"

"At home," I say.

"And how did you get here?"

"Dad grabbed our bug-out bags, and we took off."

We can still hear Dad and Freddy arguing upstairs. I think he's trying to distract me when he asks me again, "Do you like it up here?"

"That's a stupid question." And it is a stupid question.

"Because I should know the answer?"

"Because the answer should be obvious to anyone."

"I like it here." He seems to be sincere.

"Because you have nowhere else to go."

"Because it's nice. Be careful taking things for granted. One day they could all be gone."

"I've already learned that lesson," I educate him.

Upstairs, Dad's pacing slows, and his voice gets quieter. I want to sneak up there and listen just outside the door, but I've got my directions. I need to stand guard. Or sit guard at least. If the man tries to get loose from the chair, I'm to put a bullet in his chest.

"My daughter's here," Dad says, barely loud enough for me to hear. "I've done everythin' in my power to make this a safe place for her. I'm not going to jeopardize that because you owe some stranger a debt."

"He's tied up. Okay? Take this time to mull it over. Take the night. What's left of it."

The floorboards warp and I can tell Dad has walked over to the window. He's probably looking out at the tree line. He does that a lot. No idea why, though. There's never anything new to see.

Freddy continues, "Eventually, someone else may stumble upon the cabin. Maybe someone with bad intentions. And what then? Like Roger said, strength in numbers."

"What do you think your dad's gonna do?" Roger asks me. He doesn't sound afraid. Doesn't sound cocky either. He speaks like he's made a business proposition that he's waiting to have accepted.

"I don't know."

"I'm not an evil man."

"I don't know that either. Other than Freddy and my father, I can't speak to anyone else's intentions, especially not someone I've met only an hour earlier in the middle of the night."

"That's where trust comes in," he says.

"My Dad would say, that's where risk comes in."

The door to Dad's room swings open, and Freddy follows him out. Roger looks up at them walking beside the railing. He smiles, Dad just glares back.

"Joy," Dad says. He rarely uses my name. I look at him, waiting for him to finish. "Go on to bed."

I stand and head for my room, passing Dad and Freddy as they make their way down. I know better than to argue. Stopping at my door, I watch to see what he'll do next. He doesn't even turn to look at me when he says, "I said get to bed."

I enter my room, rifle still in hand, and I close the door behind me. Pressing my ear to the wood, I listen to every syllable the men utter. I'm sure Dad knows I'm listening. There's not much way around it. I may hear terrible things, but that doesn't mean he has to let me see it when it's in his control to shield me.

"I'm gonna humor you both for the night," I hear him say. "But if I wake up to find Roger here out of his bindings, Freddy, you better have blown your own damned head off."

The amount of give in the stairs tells me Dad's coming back up. He's heavier than Freddy by at least twenty pounds. Dad's not a fat man. Not out of shape by any means. But Freddy, he's what some may call scrawny. Sometimes I wonder if his big bushy beard weighs more than the rest of him.

"Warren," Roger says. There's a pause and I imagine Dad turning to look down over the railing at him tied up in the chair. "Thank you." And then Dad's footsteps resume, heading down the hall toward his bedroom.

I don't hear him close his door.

Sliding back into bed, I pull the blankets over me. I lie on my side facing the door, cradling my rifle like a stuffed animal.

I wonder if I'll be able to fall asleep tonight.

I wonder if any of us will.

5

———

I'm still awake when Dad knocks on my door.

"Breakfast."

I come down the stairs to find Dad and Freddy sitting at the table drinking coffee and eating canned vegetables and elk steaks. It's the kill from yesterday—the one I shot.

Dressed in my usual camouflage attire, sitting on my knees in the wet soil, I looked at the buck down the sight of my .30-06, unwilling to do what I knew had to be done. It just stood there, grazing, filling its stomach to survive. Unfortunately, that's exactly what we needed to do as well. I had been crying. Not sobbing or anything. Just soft crying.

After it was done, I ran my fingers through its fur for a long while. Dad said nothing. He let me work through the emotions, knowing the next part would be even tougher for me. The dressing.

Standing beside the table I try to pretend the meat Dad and Freddy are chewing isn't the same creature I'd gutted and cleaned.

"Morning," Freddy says.

"Morning," I echo.

Dad motions to a plate he has prepared for me and I sit down beside him to eat.

"Isn't anyone going to ask me how I slept?" Roger's comment makes me grin. I try to hide it, but I know Dad saw.

"You seem rather light-hearted for a man taped to a chair," Dad says.

"Just optimistic."

I eat, and with a sheepish tone, purposefully muffled by the food in my mouth, I ask, "Do I get to hear what happened?"

Freddy looks to Dad, who already heard the story last night. He hesitates a moment before giving approval.

Freddy straightens up before saying, "Well. I was on my way back from the—"

He pauses, not wanting to say the name of wherever it is he goes to visit. Dad won't ever tell me where he goes, either. But he always comes back with a different smell. So floral and sweet it almost makes me gag.

"...And suddenly I see these flashing lights behind me on the road."

"A Lawman," I say.

"Yeah. Pulled me over, asking for my papers. Of course, I don't have any papers to show."

None of us do.

"And when the Lawman confirmed it, he just pulled out his nightstick and started beating the shit outta me. I think he fractured some bones in my face."

There's the explanation for the bruises.

"Had he just cuffed me and tossed me into the back of his vehicle the way he was supposed to, he probably would have survived," Freddy says. As soon as that word leaves his mouth, he regrets it. *Survived.* Spoiler alert. That Lawman's dead now. So which one of them killed him?

Freddy glances at Dad, clears his throat and keeps going. "Well, eventually he started tiring of kicking my ass and went and leaned against the side of my car. Asshole just stood there and lit up a cigarette."

He pauses there, and I can tell the image is burned into his brain.

"Then these headlights appeared on the horizon and the Lawman saunters over to his squad car, reaches in through the window and flips on the red and blues." And Freddy clicks his tongue. "A Jeep pulls up alongside and the Lawman, showing the size of his dick—er, uh excuse me, Joy—he puts his hand on his sidearm."

He's always so fidgety. Poor Freddy. I know I make him uncomfortable. He still thinks of me as if I'm a little kid that he's got to watch his mouth around. Half the time, he doesn't even know which words he should hold back. Can't say he doesn't try, though.

"The passenger window of the mystery vehicle rolls down, and the Lawman says 'Help you?' but the driver doesn't answer. And the rain's just fucking pounding down on us. The Lawman says, 'Got your papers on ya? That's why you're stoppin', ain't it,' but the driver still doesn't respond. So the Lawman draws his pistol and demands the driver show him his papers. That's when the driver,"—and Freddy points at Roger—"Finally answered him. 'I have them right here, officer,' he said. Then the Lawman tells him to move along, and Roger does, and leaves me there alone."

I look at Roger to read his face. Did he really just leave him there?

"Then the Lawman, he walks back over to me and presses my face back down in the mud with the toe of his boot. 'Hear that, boy? Fucker back there'—ah shit, I mean—'guy back there stopped to show me his papers. I had to all but beat your ass to death to get yours. And what do I find? Fuckin' for'—Christ, sorry, Joy." He turns to Dad, who shakes his head like an annoyed father figure.

Freddy clears his throat again, takes a drink, "He says, 'And what do I find? A forgery. You know what that means, right? Means your ass is headed back to town. Headed back to the camp.' And there I am, all helpless, lying on the ground, and I'm pleading with him to just let me go. 'If you ain't got no papers, you ain't makin' it outta the state,' he tells me."

It's one hell of a story.

"Then we see headlights again, the Jeep, speeding back toward us. The Lawman pulled his pistol but before he could fire off a shot, the Jeep was right there." Freddy claps his hands together dramatically and the smack echoes through the cabin. "The front bumper clipped his leg as he attempted to dive out of the way, and this asshole goes spinning through the air and hits the ground right next to me."

I can't help but grin when I glance at Roger.

"The Jeep skids to a halt and Roger emerges from the driver's seat. And the Lawman's lying there, howling, gripping his fucked up leg."

Freddy doesn't catch himself on that one. I've never seen him this animated before.

"Then Roger picks up the asshole's pistol. So I pull myself up, and the Lawman's reaching for his shoulder radio to call for backup, and I just smash him right in the face with his own nightstick. 'You have your papers, officer.' And I hit him again, right in the nose, and blood spurts out like a goddamned geyser."

My eyes are so wide they hurt. Surely Freddy's exaggerating here. I've never seen him do anything like that. Dad, yes. But Freddy? My gaze shifts back to Roger, expecting him to be shaking his head in disagreement, but he's just sitting there listening, a modest expression across his face.

"And Roger, he's standing by, watching me as I wallop this guy, all calm, like he's standing in line at the grocery store. He didn't even react at all when I stomped on the Lawman's neck."

Whoa.

"What?" I ask.

"Fuck. I didn't mean to tell you that part." Freddy shoots Dad a worried look.

"You stepped on his neck?" I ask.

He briefly considers denying it, but what good would it do? He already said it. "Yeah. Had to."

"That's right," Dad says. "We don't need anyone comin' around lookin' for revenge."

It makes sense. Still wasn't what I was expecting to hear. Thought he was going to tell me he shot the guy. Stomping on his neck? Jesus.

"Anyway. I thank Roger for stopping, and he says he's always willing to help a man in need."

Dad looks over at Roger. He's still making up his mind about this man.

"But now my car's made," Freddy says. "Lawman had already called it in. So we both hop in his Jeep and get the hell outta there."

"You took quite the beating," I say.

"I've had worse." It sounds cliché when he says it, but I know it's true. Isn't much of a way around it these days.

Dad's not the biggest conversationalist, and when Freddy's in his proximity, neither is he. I figure it's now or never to get the entire story.

"Where were you headed?" I ask Roger.

"That was my first question to Freddy," Roger says. "Didn't wanna share that with me, of course."

"You asked me if I had a plan, and I asked you if you had one—"

Roger cuts him off. "And I said, 'Yeah, mine's looking for someone else who's got one.'"

Freddy chuckles. "He was planning on leachin'. And when he saw me get my ass beat on the side of the road, figured I might be someone he could leach off. That's why he stopped."

Dad nods as he chews.

"I stopped to be a good samaritan. If I could leach, it would've been a bonus."

"Yeah." Freddy says. "And I appreciated him stopping and all but—"

"Stopping and saving your life," Roger corrects.

"And saving me, but I told him I can't have anyone tagging along."

Roger grins as he says, "At which point I reminded Freddy that his car was marked. He was riding in my vehicle now, so if anyone was tagging along, it was him."

"Anyhow, he says to me he knows a man with a plan when he sees one and wants to know where I'm headed. And I tell him it's somewhere I'm not welcome to bring along partners."

Roger tries to adjust in the chair. "That's when I know he's got a haven."

"I said, I *know* someone who's got one. And that someone isn't the sharing type."

"And so Freddy says that although he realizes I saved his life, he can't take me with him to your father's cabin. And I kindly explain to him that outside the camps, you can do whatever you want so long as you don't get caught. I told him, in this state of vulnerability I say you can, and insist you will, take me with you to your friend's haven."

They look at each other. "And he follows it up with 'And I'd prefer that my insistence will suffice.' As if that isn't at all threatening."

My gaze shifts between the three men. Roger trying to sell himself as a good person, Freddy trying to justify his actions, and Dad judging them both. He already heard this all from Freddy once. Would Roger's additional comments be enough to persuade him?

Freddy says, "I won't lie. The look in Roger's eyes in that moment sent a shudder down my spine. I've been in a lot of scrapes, come up against several dangerous men, but his presence outweighed any I'd encountered before. He was just—brimming with intensity."

"Brimming with intensity?" Roger's tone is mocking.

"You got charisma, I guess."

Dad takes another bite of the steak and stares at Roger as he chews the mouthful. "You didn't answer her question," Dad says.

"What?" Roger asks.

"Where were you headed?"

"Anywhere, Warren. Anywhere safe."

Dad wipes his mouth and looks straight at me. "I'm not against helping others. You know that. Before all this I was… but things aren't the same as back then. I have my concerns, but Freddy's vouchin' for this man." I'm left speechless for a long moment after he asks, "What do you think?"

What do I think?

Up to this point, it's all been about following Dad's direction. Do what he says so we can survive. No questions. Just act and act quick. Now here we are, sitting at the table like some makeshift family, and he's asking *my* opinion about the stranger.

"I—"

All three of them are looking at me.

I force a brave face and answer. "We don't have time to spoon feed him all his meals or tilt his head back to give him water every few hours. There's work to be done. And we can't rightly shoot him now that he's unarmed and all. Freddy trusts him. So I want to trust him too. I think for now, till he gives us reason to do otherwise, we cut him loose."

Somehow Roger is smiling bigger than he was before. "I couldn't be happier with your vote of confidence."

Dad reads my eyes to be sure I've spoken truthfully.

"Alright then," he says and looks at Roger. "But make no mistake, if you do anythin'—anythin' that makes me uneasy, or leads me to believe you got any malicious motives, I'll gun you down armed or not."

"I assure you, my motives are sincere."

Dad nods at Freddy, who gets up from the table, and, using his steak knife, cuts Roger free from the chair.

Rubbing his wrists, Roger stands to stretch. He looks at the three of us one at a time, taking a moment to make eye contact individually. "Thank you. All of you. I promise to do my part around here."

Freddy pats him on the back and sits back down at the table to finish his meal.

"Come nightfall though, your ass goes back in the chair," Dad says. "I wanna be able to sleep with both eyes closed."

"Understood."

"Now...," Dad clears his throat as if mustering the strength to show more hospitality. "You want some breakfast?"

6

Dad's at his modest wooden desk listening to the police scanner with his oversized headphones, the kind that plug in with a curly cord. Static sounds. That's all he ever hears. And that's a good thing. I glance at him through the window from my seat on the porch in one of the two rocking chairs—Dad says he made them as a young man.

Freddy sits in the second, smoking one of his hand-rolled cigarettes. We both subtly watch Roger, who's standing a few feet away, staring out into the woods, holding his cup of tea.

"What are you looking for?" Freddy asks.

"I'm not looking for anything. I'm enjoying the scenic view."

"It's just a bunch of trees. How's that qualify as a scenic view?"

"I'm used to a very different setting, Freddy. This right here, it's a scenic view. Trust me."

I thought it was beautiful when we first got up here. Now, after some time has passed, I would be fine with never seeing this place again. But I know that's not reality. I know we're stuck here. Leaving this land is a death sentence, Dad likes to tell me.

"Dad's Grandpa built this cabin," I tell Roger.

"That right?"

"Picked this spot specifically. You know why?"

Roger looks around as though he's going to see something he previously missed. "Because it's isolated?"

"It's in the center of wildlife migratory path. Elk, mule deer, whitetail. They all pass by here throughout the year. Dad's grandpa chose this spot for survival. You can build a cabin, stock it with canned food and bottled water, but sooner or later, without access to fresh water, game or a garden, you're dead. Preparedness is the only hero we have."

I get up from my chair and poke my head through the door. "Dad?" He can't hear me with the headphones on. I enter and touch his shoulder gently, trying not to startle him. He looks up at me, peeling one of the speakers from his ear.

"I'm gonna head down to the stream to catch some rainbow for dinner," I tell him.

He looks at Freddy and Roger through the window. "Take the two of them with you. Make sure the new guy knows how to hold his own."

"I'll show him."

I stroll back outside and ask Roger, "Can you fly fish?"

"No."

"You need to learn. Gear's down here by the stream." I motion for him to join. "Dad wants you to come too, Freddy." Freddy drops his cigarette and uses the toe of his boot to crush it out, then immediately cleans up the butt, dusting the ash away. He knows how Dad gets if he leaves a mess.

I walk into the woods, rifle slung over my shoulder. Roger follows me through the tree line and a moment later I hear Freddy hustling up behind us, no doubt having clarified instructions with Dad.

"There's only two sets," I say.

"I'll just watch," Freddy replies, adjusting the pistol in his waistband.

Down along the bank, I show Roger the waders and we each pull a pair on. I tie a fly onto his line and we make our way out into the middle of the shallow stream. I cast upstream, and he tries to mimic my movements, but I can tell he has no idea what he's doing.

"Am I doing this correctly?"

I lie. "Looking good so far. Just keep gathering the line." The flies pass us and continue downstream. "You want it to move naturally with the current. Don't want it to drag."

I glance over at him and can tell he's concentrating. "Lift your line. Flip it back upstream like this," I tell him as I mend my line. He attempts to imitate my movement again. After a few tries, he gets it.

"Alright, recast it." And we both cast upstream.

He's smiling. He's the only person I've seen smile in over a year.

"I can't remember the last time I was this relaxed," he says.

"This is where we'd come to get away from everything. Even before the Shit. Something about letting the water run past my legs—like everything in the world is rushing past, but I'm standing still, safe from it all." I look over at him. "Recast."

Freddy watches us from the base of the tree he's leaning against. I'm not sure if he's being so quiet because he's got nothing to say, or because it hurts his face too much to speak. That Lawman sure did a number.

"You good?" I ask, and he just nods.

Roger is getting the hang of it now. Still no bites, but his form is improving by the minute. I still have some unanswered questions, but I can tell he's content standing here in the river with me in silence. I'll let him enjoy it.

As I take a step to wade deeper toward the center, I lose my footing over a slick stone beneath the current, and topple sideways into the stream. The water had felt cool through the waders, but as it pours in, soaking my pants and sweater, I feel just how icy it really is. Roger's hand clamps around my arm and pulls me back up almost immediately.

"You alright?"

"Yeah," I answer, still regaining my composure. He helps me to the shore, and I can see the concern in Freddy's eyes clocking Roger's hand still holding me just above the elbow.

"Get your sweater off," Roger says. He's already unbuttoning his long-sleeve flannel.

"What?"

Freddy approaches.

"And your shirt. We can't let your body temp drop. It's cold out here. Don't want you catching something we don't have meds for."

I'm shivering. I know he's right, but the thought of removing my clothes in front of the two men is the last thing I want to do.

"Come on, quick," he says. He's stripped off the flannel now, holding it out for me to take from him.

"Hold on a sec," Freddy speaks up.

I turn my back to them and quickly pull my sweater and shirt up and over my head, then snag the flannel from his hand and pull it over my body, buttoning it up as hastily as I can manage. With the last button done up I turn back around expecting to see them awkwardly looking at the sky or diverting their attention to the trees.

But the men are staring directly at one another. It's the first time I've seen Freddy look at Roger this way. He looks surprised—no, afraid maybe. Why's he looking at him like that?

Roger is only a couple feet away with his back to me. I can't see his expression, but the rest of his stance tells me he's preparing himself for something.

"Why didn't you tell me?" Freddy asks.

"You know why," Roger says.

What the hell are they talking about?

"This changes things."

"It doesn't need to."

"If Warren finds out—if he sees that," Freddy says, and he points his finger at Roger, at something on his arm that I can't see from where I'm standing. "...he'll kill you."

"What's going on?" I ask. They both look at me, and as Roger turns to face me, I see it. A tattoo on his left shoulder. It's a skull wearing a beret, with a dagger stabbing upward through the jaw and some sort of viper coiling around the hilt and blade.

A military tattoo.

A million thoughts run through my mind, but no words make it past my lips. I know what the military did. I know the part they played in the Shit. Is that why he's here? Is that why he tricked Freddy into bringing him here? To find us? To bring us in?

He sees my eyes shift to my rifle propped up against a nearby tree behind him. He knows what I'm thinking.

"I can explain."

"No explanation's gonna satisfy Warren," Freddy says.

"I saved your life, Freddy."

"And maybe there's a reason you did that other than self-preservation."

Roger shakes his head.

"Step down by the water," I tell him.

"Joy—"

"Step down by the water!" I can barely believe the sound of my voice as it comes out of me, and by the looks on their faces, neither can Roger and Freddy.

"You don't need your rifle," Roger says. "Let me just explain."

"You can explain down by the water."

He's about to try again, but bites his tongue and moves slowly down the bank. I hurry over to my rifle and raise it to my shoulder. His hands shoot up defensively. "Joy, please."

"Why are you here?"

"I told you. I'm looking for a haven."

"No. You're a soldier. You don't need one. Try again."

"I *was* a soldier. Not anymore."

I glance at Freddy to see if he's buying it. I can tell he isn't convinced. He's just standing there at a safe distance, glaring, his fingers grazing the grip of the pistol still tucked into his jeans.

"Go on," I say to Roger.

"I'm a deserter."

"Why should we believe that?"

"I saved Freddy. From a cop. And I stood by as he killed him."

"Standing idly by while someone kills someone else isn't helping to convince me."

Freddy finally draws his gun.

"You want help, Freddy? Then go get Dad."

"I can't leave you alone out here with him," Freddy says.

I nod. Strength in numbers. "Then we march him back."

"Listen. Warren—your dad, he's quick to react. He won't give me an opportunity to explain before he shoots me."

"Well, we're giving you the opportunity and you're wasting it." I shrug my shoulders to tug back on the long sleeves of the flannel that keep sliding down over my hands.

"I deserted my unit when I saw what they were capable of doing. What they were *comfortable* doing. I'm not like them. I'm not... I'm not an evil man."

"Then what are you?" I ask.

"I'm just a man. I'm not here to hurt anyone. We don't need to tell your dad about the tattoo. Alright? We can keep it between the three of us. I don't touch a gun. You both keep your eyes on me if it makes you feel better. But I get the opportunity to prove to you I'm on the up and up."

"And what about when we're asleep?"

"Your dad made it clear that I go back in the chair at night. Right? So that takes care of that."

"We don't have any reason to trust you," I tell him.

He lowers his hands, his gaze falling to the dirt in defeat. Then with what I can only understand as a man giving it his last go, tears welled in his eyes, he looks back up at me and says, "I saved his life."

"*I* don't have any reason to trust you."

He bites the side of cheek, smiling through the tears, and says, "But you can choose to."

I try to read him, searching for a crack in the façade, but something tells me he's speaking true. I know that he's dangerous. I know that if I wasn't holding my rifle he could easily overpower me, maybe even me *and* Freddy—soldiers are trained in hand to hand combat, right?—but even though this man had taken Freddy hostage, held a gun to his head and forced his way into our cabin, and bares a tattoo representing all I've been groomed to hate, there's something about him I want to trust.

You can choose to. My head cocks involuntarily and I'm not sure if he repeated himself or if his words merely echoed in my head. He stares at me, looking vulnerable, like a man about to be executed. And that's what he is right now. He's awaiting his sentence. And I'm the judge... again.

Freddy takes a step toward me. "Joy—"

"Stop," I say. And he does.

I look at the tattoo and for a moment I could almost swear that I saw the serpent constrict tighter around the dagger. I close my eyes and shake it off.

"You surrendered your gun to my dad," I say as I lower my rifle. "I'll pay you the same respect. Because I want to believe you." The relief that spreads across his face is unmistakable. "Maybe I have to believe you."

"Thank you," he says. It's becoming his catch-phrase.

"Joy," Freddy starts in. "If your dad—"

"What, Freddy? Who do you think he's going to blame? You think it'll stop at Roger? You don't think he'll have something against you for bringing him here, for vouching for him?"

Freddy grits his teeth. He knows I'm right. Best-case scenario if Dad finds out Roger has a military tattoo: he kicks Freddy out of the cabin. Most likely scenario: he buries Freddy out back so he can ensure he doesn't retaliate for the exiling.

"Better put your flannel back on then," Freddy tells Roger.

7

———

I wring out my shirt and sweater. I don't have to tell them to turn around as I change back into the damp clothes. Roger pulls his flannel back on and we make our way back toward the cabin. I bring up the rear, rifle in hand, with Freddy leading the way and Roger between us.

A faint rustling sound catches my attention and instinctively, I stop. Could be a deer. Or a rabbit. The men stop as well. I survey the landscape, trying to zero in on the exact origin of the noise.

I hear it again. Moving forward cautiously, my rifle at the ready, I hear Roger call my name in a whisper. I ignore him. He says it a bit louder. I keep moving.

The terrain slopes downward in front of me, and I lean out forward to see what lies below. Something several feet down the hill is moving lightly in the brush. Raising my rifle into firing position, I look through the scope to get a better view.

Oh, God. Taking a deep breath, I carefully make my way down the hill, keeping the rifle aimed and ready. I hear Freddy and Roger following softly behind. Approaching the origin of the sound, I point the barrel at the injured man lying in the brush, a deep wound on his abdomen, blood draining into the soil.

"Who are you?" I demand.

The man looks up at me, his face smeared with blood, his breathing shallow. He tries to speak, but his voice is too quiet for me to make out. Freddy and Roger reach me and take in the sight. I look the man over to be sure he's of no threat.

"Ah, hell," Freddy says. "It's Leonard."

I want to ask how Freddy knows him, how this *Leonard* found his way up here, but before I can, he tries again to tell me something. I kneel beside his face, trying to listen as Freddy scrambles down beside us.

The man's eyes are blurry, drifting from side to side as if in a trance. "Warren Bellows," he says. "I need Warren Bellows."

I pull back. "How do you know Warren Bellows?"

"Please." His voice is a whisper. "Tell him—" His breathing slows.

"Tell him what?"

His eyes stop drifting and settle to one side, and he wheezes out, "They're coming."

I run.

Sprinting through the trees at full speed, I'm afraid, but focused. If Roger and Freddy are following me, I do not know. Emerging into the clearing where the cabin waits, I throw open the door and bolt inside.

Dad, startled by the state of my entry, turns from his radio desk. He sees the look in eyes. He knows what it means.

A moment later we're running together, both with our rifles, back through the forest, back to the hill where Roger and Freddy are waiting.

The injured man has expired, laying dead in the brush. "It's Leonard," Freddy says.

"Damnit," Dad snarls through his teeth.

Roger is inspecting the body. "Friend of yours?"

"Told him where to find the cabin on the off chance he could get outta town like the rest of us."

Roger's fingertips find the bullet hole in the flesh.

"Let's get him back to the cabin," Dad says, and he lifts the man's legs while Freddy grabs the body under the arms. Roger offers to help but Dad turns him down, so he walks along awkwardly behind them as they carry the corpse back toward the cabin.

I stare down the hill, deeper into the woods as the dead man's last words echoed through my mind. *They're coming.*

8

Leonard's body lies on the kitchen table covered in the white sheet from Dad's bed. Freddy sits at the table, his elbows planted, his face in his palms.

I come down the stairs after quickly changing into dry clothes and Roger, leaning against the kitchen sink, glances over at me. Dad finally breaks the silence.

"One more time. What exactly did he say to you?"

"I told you. He said 'they're coming.'"

"But he didn't specify who," Freddy says.

"Did he need to?" Roger asks.

"This is fucking great."

"Just because he was bein' hunted doesn't mean we are. Coulda just been marauders." Dad is inspecting his rifle.

"We'd be lucky if that were the case," Roger says.

Freddy looks up from his palms. "Leonard was shot. Small caliber. Whoever they are, they aren't packing heavy firepower."

"That's a rather large assumption to make, don't you think?"

I hop up onto the back of the couch. "If they tracked Leonard, they can track us. We should move to the bunker." As soon as the words come out of my mouth, I know I've made a mistake. Dad turns and glares at me.

"What bunker?" Roger asks.

"Joy," Dad says through his teeth.

I hesitate, then convincing myself that my rationalization is worth sharing, I say, "If they're still looking for him, they're going to find our trail and it's going to lead them right to us. And what then?"

Dad stands and lets the rifle rest over his shoulder. "The bunker's a last resort."

"What bunker?" Roger asks again. Dad and Freddy are silent. Roger turns to me.

"The security bunker below the cabin."

"Joy!" Dad screams at me, his grip tightening so hard around the barrel of the rifle I expected to crack.

"If you have a bunker, then let's get down there!"

"I ain't gonna lock us underground until it's absolutely necessary. Once we're in there, it's for the long haul. I ain't ready for that. *We* ain't ready for that."

Roger is already looking around the room for some sign of the bunker entrance. "We can just go down there till these people pass us by."

"And what? Let them rummage through the house? Take whatever they want? If they show up here, I'm gonna put a damned bullet in their heads. We stand our ground. We don't lock ourselves away and hide. That was the purpose of lettin' you stay here, wasn't it? So you could help defend the cabin?"

Freddy forces himself out of the chair and saunters right through the middle of Dad's and Roger's stare down. "I could use some help digging a grave," Freddy says, attempting to break them up. Roger relinquishes and follows Freddy out the front door.

Dad's hand settles on my shoulder as we watch them leave. I wait a few minutes before saying, "I'm sorry about your friend."

"Yeah."

"How did you know him?"

Dad groans as if using his memory is painful somehow. "We worked together."

"For Mom?"

"What's with the questions, Joy?" He made his way across the room and filled the kettle.

"I just thought—"

"Don't. Okay?" He lit the burner on the stove and turned to me. "You shouldn't have told him about the bunker."

"Why not?"

"Because we don't know him. Some things we just need to keep to ourselves."

Less than an hour later, we're all out back standing over the hole Freddy and Roger dug. Leonard's body is lying at the bottom, the bedsheet now removed, leaving him exposed.

Dad shovels heaps of dirt from the mound back down into the grave and Freddy asks, "You aren't going to say anything?"

"Ain't got nothin' to say."

9

Roger sits down in the chair near the kitchen table as Dad peels a length of electrical tape from the roll. Freddy, standing in the kitchen, gives him a "cheers" gesture with his teacup.

"You're still sure this is necessary?" Roger asks. Dad tapes Roger's arms and legs to the chair. "Perhaps you could reconsider, in light of recent developments."

I pour myself a glass of water as I watch. Dad gives a slight tug at Roger's extremities to make sure he's confident in his work, and without another word, walks up the stairs and closes himself in his bedroom.

Freddy shrugs, walks past Roger, patting him on the shoulder as he goes, and flops down on the couch to pass out. "Good night, Joy."

"Night, Freddy."

"Good night, Joy," Roger says.

I take a sip of my water and head upstairs, keeping my eyes on Roger as I go. He doesn't look up at me. His eyes are closed now. His breathing deep. I leave my door open a crack, so I can hear. In case something were to happen. In case I made a mistake.

My rifle waits for me in bed. I slide beneath the covers and turn my back to the nightstand, where the only remaining photograph of my mother sits in a pewter frame. I've stared at it for so many hours, hoping the image has permanently burned itself into my brain, hoping it will stay as vibrant in my mind even when it's not with me.

It's not long before I hear the snoring. *Must be Freddy.* I imagine his neck bent crooked against the arm of the couch, his mouth hanging open, his breath rustling the fatty parts inside his throat as he sleeps. I've seen him sleeping like that before, usually after a long day of knocking out a list of chores Dad's given him, or after making the long trek back to the cabin after one of his hiatuses.

I have my assumptions about where he goes. Whatever makes him come back smelling like cheap perfume must be amazing enough to risk his life each time to visit it. And if it wasn't for Roger this last time, he would have finally run out of luck.

A thunderous banging sends a surge of adrenaline through my body. I sit up in bed, both hands scooping up my rifle. It's the front door again.

I hear the moan of Dad's bedroom door opening down the hall and see him pass by my cracked door. I move silently and peer down to the second floor as Dad descends the stairs. Freddy is already up off the couch, standing apprehensibly near Roger in the chair.

"Untie me," he whispers. "Fucking, get me out of this chair."

"Shut up," Dad growls back in a hushed tone. He has his shotgun aimed at the door.

This is why I voted to let Roger stay. Not just to give him safety, but so he could help protect us as well. Whoever's on the other side of the door is... I need to get Roger out of that chair.

I sneak down the steps, strafe into the kitchen, pull a knife from the drawer and without a word, cut Roger free.

Dad hears me but keeps his sights on the front door. I pull a Colt Peacemaker from inside one of the cabinets and toss it to Roger, who catches it with ease, and quickly checks the chambers.

The pounding on the door continues, rattling the hinges. "What do you want?" Dad shouts.

"Please! You have to help me! They're after me!" It's a man's voice, scared, warbling.

"Who the hell are you?"

"Please! They're trying to kill me. You have to let me in."

"Who's trying to kill you?" Dad keeps his distance from the door.

"I don't know! Please, just let me in. Please." Dad glances at Freddy, who shakes his head. "Goddamnit! Please, I'm unarmed!"

"Warren," Roger says.

"Shut up." Dad still doesn't bother looking at him.

"What if he's telling the truth? What if he's like us?"

"He's not."

"You don't know that."

"Don't let me die out here," the Stranger shouts. "Not like this."

What if he's telling the truth? What if he really is in danger? We can't just leave him out there to die.

"Dad?" I say. He looks at Freddy a second time, but this time Freddy doesn't shake his head. This time he's uncertain what to do. Then Dad looks at me and sees the worry in my eyes.

"I'm gonna open the door," he shouts at the Stranger. "When I do, I want to see you on your knees, hands behind your head, with your back to me. If you are not in this position when I open the door, I'll put a slug through your damned neck. Do you understand me?"

"Yes! Yes! Thank you. Yes."

Dad moves in close to the door. I reach out slowly and grab the doorknob, waiting for his signal. Then he nods, and I pull the door open. The Stranger is on his knees, hands behind his head, with his back to us, just as instructed. Dad grabs him by the collar and pulls him backward into the house, throwing him onto his back on the floor as I slam the door closed.

He stares up at us, his face distorted by shaggy hair and an unkempt beard, his body hidden beneath a heavy jacket. "Thank you. Jesus, thank all of you."

"Check him," Dad says, and Freddy searches him for weapons—anything dangerous.

"I think he's clean."

"Get him up." Freddy helps the Stranger to his feet and brings him face to face with Dad. "Who the hell are you?"

"I—I don't really remember."

"What the fuck do you mean, you don't remember?" Freddy asks.

"I fell when I escaped from the Camps. Hit my head. That's what John said. Fucked me up a bit. I'm having trouble remembering much of anything before that."

"Who's John?" The Stranger turns to look at Roger for the first time.

"John. He helped me get out. Not sure if I knew him before we got locked up or not."

"Where's John now?"

"They—they killed him."

"Who?" Dad asks.

"I don't know. The men that've been chasing me." The Stranger is finally catching his breath. "Can I have some water?"

Roger pours him a glass and the Stranger chugs it and sets it down on the table. Dad moves around behind him, keeping the man centered between the lot of us.

"These men," Freddy says. "How many of them are there?"

"Three. Four maybe. They're savages."

"What do you mean, savages?"

"They killed John with a tomahawk. Disemboweled him. Chopped his arms off. Can I have some more water, please?"

Roger fills the glass again, and the Stranger takes a drink. "Thank you."

"When was that?" He's surprised to hear me speak.

"What?"

"When did they kill your friend?"

"Yesterday. Or earlier today. I don't know what time it is."

"Did you see them chasing anyone else?"

"Anyone else? What do you mean?"

Freddy steps in closer to him. "What the fuck do you think she means? Were they chasing anyone else? Did you *see* anyone else?"

"No. I don't think so. John and I, we were hiding out after we got free. We had just lied down out in the woods when we started hearing these noises. Like chanting or something. We weren't sure what it was, so we put out the fire so we wouldn't be seen. But it was too late. They'd already noticed us. Fucking came out of the trees like a bunch of psychopaths. Swinging axes and waving branches around their heads, hooting and shouting like goddamn animals.

"We took off running. Put a bit of distance between us and them, but one had a pistol. John got shot in the leg, made me leave him behind. Said he wasn't going to make it. No sense in both of us dying, he said. I argued, but he wouldn't let me stay. I watched from some bushes when they caught up to him. They laughed when they did it. They fucking laughed."

The Stranger was on the verge of tears as he recounted his story, and for a moment all of us were silent as we visualized.

"Where are they now?"

"I don't know. I ran through the night."

"How did you find us?" Dad asks.

"I just stumbled across you. Saw the cabin when I was running through the trees. God. Thank you for letting me in."

As the Stranger lifts the glass to take another drink, something beneath his sleeves catches Roger's attention. I see him cock his head slightly, then he sits down at the table with the Stranger.

"They're probably tracking me. If they can't in the dark, then they'll wait till the morning. Either way, they could pick up my trail." He looks around at the three of us. "Do you have more weapons than this? More ammo?"

"You said there were only four of them?" Dad asks.

"I think that's all there are. Yeah."

"And only one has a gun?"

"From what I could tell."

"And these men, they were just roaming the mountainside, looking for victims?" The skepticism in Freddy's voice is palpable.

"I don't know what they were doing before they found us. All I know is they hacked my friend apart and tried to do the same to me."

I move to the window and peer out casually through the blinds. Nothing but darkness. I can't even see the trees.

"You said you were in the Camps before this." Roger says.

"Yeah."

"And you *escaped*?"

"Yeah. I don't really remember much, like I said. Just that I hit my head. Falling from the fence maybe."

I can tell Dad is curious about where Roger is going with his line of questioning.

"But you were interned there?" Roger continues.

"Yeah." The Stranger takes a long drink of water. Roger stands up from the table and walks over to Dad, whispering something in his ear. I see Dad's jaw tighten. "Is something wrong?" the Stranger asks.

Dad walks around and sits down across the table from the Stranger in the chair Roger had just vacated. "You wouldn't be bullshittin' us, would ya?"

"What do you mean?"

"Our friend was recently found shot dead out in the woods. Could be that it was these savages you've been goin' on about that killed him."

The Stranger nods. "That's a likely bet."

"Or could be you."

The Stranger straightens up. "I'm no killer. Don't even know how to use a gun. If it's true what you say about your friend getting shot, I have no doubt in my mind it was the same men that killed John."

"You think so?"

"Absolutely."

Dad nods slowly. "How about you take that jacket off?"

"My jacket? Your man already searched me."

"Take it off," Dad says.

Roger presses the Peacemaker to the back of the Stranger's head. "Take off the jacket."

"Did I miss something? I'm no threat, folks." Roger pokes his head aggressively with the barrel. "Alright. Okay."

The Stranger shrugs the heavy jacket off his shoulders and pulls his arms from the sleeves, letting it fall to the floor behind him. All our weapons are back up, pointing at the Stranger. We can all see it. The military tattoo on his forearm—a skull wearing a beret, with a dagger piercing upward through the jawbone, and a snake coiling around the hilt.

Just like Roger's.

"What kind of military man doesn't know how to use a gun?" Dad asks. The Stranger sits contemplating his options. He knows the jig is up. "Let's start from the get-go. Who the hell are you?"

The layers of sheepishness and exasperation wash away from the Stranger's body, and as though he is speaking in a completely new voice, he says, "The odds of your survival are too slim to even measure. Your only play is to hand your weapons over to me."

Dad looks at Roger. "That cockiness sounds familiar." Then to Freddy, "Tie him up."

Freddy grabs the roll of electrical tape and begins securing the Stranger to the chair. "I'll ask again," Dad says. "Who are you?"

"Just a man doing his duty."

"Where are your friends?"

"Outside. All around."

I peek out the blinds again, expecting to see the cabin surrounded, but still the only thing to be seen is blackness.

"How many?" Dad asks. The Stranger grins. "How many, damn it!"

"You know what I said before, about that group of savages? That wasn't all a lie. We did come across some boys. Fucking cannibals. 'Least that's what they looked like. Stomped their heads in with our boots. Of course, that was after we cut their jugulars out. No way we'd be able to get men like that back to the Camps. Too much trouble. More than it's worth. Question for you is, how much trouble do you really wanna give us?"

Dad chuckles lightly. "I respect your courage. Soldier to the end. But here's the thing about us. We're not a group of half-cocked man eaters. We're survivors. We'll do whatever we have to in order to stay out of those government camps. Now, how many of you are—"

"Twenty-three."

Dad smiles and shakes his head. "I don't think so."

"Doesn't really matter what you think," the Stranger says.

Dad turns to me, puts a hand on my shoulder and tells me to go upstairs. I try to debate the importance of me staying, but he isn't having it. "Joy. I need you to go upstairs. Now." The way he's talking, the eerie calm in his voice, nothing good ever follows it.

I do as he says. Making my way to the top of the stairs, I look back down at everyone. He glares up at me with an expression that says, *Get your ass in your room.*

I close the door harder than I should. Not quite a slam, but forceful enough to get my point across.

10

———

I only wait a minute or two before I silently turn the knob and inch my bedroom door back open. Dad is rifling through one of the cabinet drawers while Roger and Freddy stand behind the Stranger on either side of the chair.

Dad approaches them with a metal spatula. "You gonna grill me some burgers?" the Stranger asks, and Dad swings the spatula like a flyswatter, smacking the man across the cheek, slicing just below his cheekbone. "Fuck!"

Without hesitation, Dad hits him across the other cheek, then again across the first. The three thin cuts begin to leak blood.

"You're a scout," Dad says. "You come around, get yourself inside the cabin to get a good idea of what you're all up against. Then you signal your buddies and they storm in here to take us out. That's how it works, right?"

He raises the spatula high above his head, then brings it down across the Stranger's face, slashing his eye. The Stranger screams out in pain, his eyes squeezing closed, blood running out from between his eyelids.

"Right?" Dad screams.

"Fuck you!"

I wince as Dad uppercuts the man with the spatula, then tosses it aside. "Hold his eye open," he says to Roger. "The good one." And Dad is back at the cabinet, rummaging.

"What are you going to do?" Roger asks.

"That's a question he should be askin', not you. Hold his damned eye open."

"We don't need to do this, Warren. He's not gonna talk. You know that."

Dad pulls a metal skewer out from the drawer and holds it up for the Stranger to see. "Freddy. Hold his eye open." Freddy doesn't hesitate. He grabs the Stranger under the chin with one hand to keep him from squirming, then with his other, grabs the side of the Stranger's face, using his thumb and index finger to hold open the lids.

"We need him alive." Roger gestures at him. "He's our only insurance against the others."

"What do you think we're gonna do? Ransom him? Trade his life for ours? 'Here's your friend back—now will you leave us alone?'"

"Torturing him isn't going to get us anywhere!"

"You disagree with what I'm doin'? Then don't watch." Dad approaches the Stranger, pointing the skewer at him like a fencer holding his foil.

"Warren!" Roger yells.

"Don't you forget where you are! This is my goddamned house, not yours. And I'll decide the fate of every sonuvabitch who enters it. This man came here to kill us. He came here to put us in the damned ground! Now you march your ungrateful ass up that goddamn staircase and keep your mouth shut until I'm done with what I'm about to do."

The Stranger looks up at Roger, the only person keeping him alive at the moment.

"This is a tipping point, Warren. Understand that," Roger warns.

"Walk away now, or your ass is next!"

Roger looks at Freddy. He's standing strong, ready to see it through to the end with Dad. I can tell he wants to say more, to keep trying to persuade them, but he relents and heads to the staircase. I back away from the door and hear him knock gently. As I pull it open the rest of the way, he joins me.

"You alright?" he asks. I just nod at him. "It's gonna be okay."

"You don't have to lie to me." I close the door most of the way, leaving a gap again to see out. Roger sits on the edge of my bed.

"You shouldn't watch," he says quietly.

"You're not my dad."

"That's very true."

Below us, Dad moves in close with the skewer, pointing the sharpened tip directly at the Stranger's open eye. The man struggles to move, but Freddy holds his head like a vice.

"Hold him still," Dad says.

The skewer glides slowly toward the Stranger's dilated pupil.

"Well?" Dad asks. I know the Stranger wants to scream. He wants to beg. But he can't. He won't. "Then to hell with you."

My hands fly up, covering my face as Dad jams the skewer into the Stranger's eye. I hear him scream in agony, jerking back and forth, trying to free himself from the chair. I peek out between my fingers and see the skewer jiggling side to side as he thrashes. Freddy releases him and backs away.

"You come into my house?!" Dad screams. "My house!" I can't take my eyes off the scene. Even as Dad pulls the chef's knife from the drawer and stomps over to the Stranger. I try to prepare myself for what is about to come, taking a deep breath and holding it.

Dad stabs the knife into the man's gut. He rips it back out, then immediately stabs him again. The second time he pulls it out, the blade slings a long strand of crimson across the room. Dad stabs again, and again more crimson spurts out.

Again. And again. And again. Until the Stranger is still and silent.

Dad takes a few steps back, leaving the knife protruding from the man's chest. Freddy looks at him, his hands and arms covered in blood. Red slathered across his shirt and pants, trying to catch his breath, Dad notices his gaze and stares back.

My hands gradually lower from my face and cradle the door knob. I push it closed as quietly as I can. I've seen enough. I've seen it all.

11

———

I sleep hard the rest of the night. The adrenaline-filled horror drained everything from me. I don't even remember lying down in my bed. Maybe I didn't. Maybe I passed out and someone put me here. Roger.

I sit up and he's standing outside my open door, looking down over the railing to the first floor, an arc of sunlight shining in above him from the peaked windows.

What time is it?

Dad didn't call me for breakfast as usual. I don't think I could eat, anyway.

Roger notices I'm awake. He shoots me a half smile then turns back to whatever he's watching below.

I pull myself out of bed and walk over beside him. He's still got the Peacemaker tucked into his belt. Freddy's at the kitchen table, chewing on cold elk steak, a rifle beside his plate like a piece of silverware. Dad's at his desk, headphones over his ears, listening to the police scanner.

They're all waiting.

It's so quiet that the dull clicks of the scanner knob sound like gunshots. Dad scrolls slowly through the channels, searching for an in-use frequency.

Roger gestures back to my bedroom. At my .30-06. Everyone else has their weapon at the ready, so I shouldn't have needed the hint.

I snag it and head down the stairs to pour myself some water. Even though the floor's been recently mopped, I can still smell a sour, irony scent in the air. Freddy avoids eye contact as I pass him on my way to the fridge, and while I stand there and drink my water, he keeps his head low.

Dad must have told him to keep his mouth shut about last night when I'm in the room. As if I didn't witness the whole thing.

It wasn't even the first time I saw Dad kill someone. He attacked us for our food, or weapons, or maybe just because. It had been shortly after we escaped the city. I remember the patch he wore on his jacket, one of the hate groups. Can't remember which one. There's so many. That guy had been armed, though.

Was last night murder then?

It's not like the courts are around anymore to put someone on trial, right? So does it matter?

Leaning against the counter, I observe them. I don't want to talk about last night, anyway. They can all keep silent for all I care.

Click. Dad listens.

Click. He adjusts the headphones.

Click.

Using my middle finger, I lift one of the shutter planks just high enough for me to peer out. As usual, it's just the trees. I finish off the glass of water, only realizing at that moment just how dry my throat had been. Dad's always telling me how important it is to stay hydrated.

Something moved among the tree line. What the hell was that? Something dark. Tall. Its head turned and its eyes glistened like cheap jewelry, the kind girls at my school used to wear.

Not its eyes. Goggles.

At first I can't look away. My gaze glued to it. And my hand begins trembling uncontrollably, enough to rattle the shutter plank, enough to get Freddy and Roger's attentions.

It's only then I'm able to look over at them. I don't need to say it. It's what they've been expecting since last night.

Dad must hear something on the scanner. An in-use frequency. His back goes rigid, and he turns to us. He pulls the headphone plug from the jack and we all hear it.

"Stand by. Wait for my signal," the voice says through the speakers.

As if it were some slow-motion scene out of a Peckinpah film, Dad leaps from his seat at the desk, shouting out words that warble through the tight room.

"Okay," the voice on the speakers says. "Take her out."

I look back through the shutters and see the dark figure raise an assault rifle in my direction.

Dad's arms wrap around me, pulling me into his chest as he barrels forward. He does a sort of half spin in the air so that we both land on our shoulders on the damp floor.

A single bullet pops through the glass, leaving a hole in the window, level with where my eyes had been peering out. Everything seems to jump back into full speed and a barrage of bullets explode into the cabin.

Freddy hits the deck while Roger takes cover in my bedroom doorway. The windows are obliterated. The wooden walls splinter with every bullet impact. It's clear there's more than one shooter.

"Stay down," Dad says before crawling across the floor on this stomach to grab his shotgun. He pulls himself up beneath one of the window frames and racks it.

"How many are there?" Freddy yells.

"At least three," Dad says.

Freddy's hands cover his head, protecting his face from all the wood chips blasting across the room.

Then the shooting stops.

Dad raises up on his knees and fires off a shot, immediately dropping back down for cover.

The front door slams open and the man I saw at the tree line stomps in. Clad completely in black, balaclava and goggles covering his face, tactical vest, belt and boots. I don't have time to take in anymore than that before he lets loose with a spray of gunfire. The sofa detonates into a storm of fluffy stuffing, while shards from the kitchen cabinets pierce through like fighter jets screaming along a cloudy day.

I see Roger lean out from my bedroom. He fans the hammer of the Peacemaker, emptying the cylinder, knocking the intruder onto his back.

Six shots dead center in the chest.

He lands right beside Dad, who presses the barrel of his shotgun to the side of the man's head. If last night hadn't been traumatic enough, this might do the trick. One second the head is there, and the next it's gone—disintegrated?

No. I'm wrong. Not gone. Everywhere. Millions of tiny bits of bone and blood and brain, showering across me. Something sharp slices into my calf, cutting through my pants, imbedding itself into the meat.

A scream escapes my lungs before I'm able to even consider stifling it. My teeth gnash and I pull my knees to my chest, still staying as low to the ground as possible. My fingers fondle at something hard, jagged... and wet. They close around the object and I yank it free from my muscle.

Bringing it up to my face, it looks like a tiny boomerang, stark white showing beneath the blood. I turn it to see it from another angle and I realize I'm holding.

A wedge of the man's cranium.

I fling it away in disgust. And the gunfire begins again.

Dad kicks the front door closed and yells, "Roger, bedroom window."

"You got more ammo for this thing?"

"Nightstand by my bed," Dad says. Roger nods, and I watch him sprint down the open hallway to Dad's room before he disappears from sight.

"Joy?"

I turn and Dad's looking right at me.

"Yeah?"

Yeah? What kind of response is that?

"You alright?" Dad asks.

I nod, though I'm not sure I am.

"Freddy?"

And Freddy looks up from the floor, his open hands still hovering over his head like little umbrellas.

"Grab your rifle off the table and get your ass over here."

I don't feel so bad now for not grabbing my .30-06 as soon as I rolled out of bed. Freddy didn't even think to grab his when people started shooting at us.

He does as he's told, like usual, and scurries over to the wall alongside Dad.

"What do you see?" Dad asks him as he reloads the shotgun from the collection of shells he has swimming around inside his cargo pockets.

"What do I *see*?"

Dad bucks his head, motioning at what's left of the window above them. "Give me some eyes."

"You want me to—"

I'm already up, my back tight to the wall, my leg hurting like hell, and I take a lightning quick glance. It's enough though. At least enough to give Dad what he needs.

"There's at least five more," I say.

Dad, surprised to see me standing there beside the window frame, doesn't respond right away. It doesn't deter him from sneering at Freddy's cowardice, however.

I hate seeing Freddy in that state, but we're all aware of the kind of man he is. They can't all be Rambo. And sometimes, those are the ones that survive the longest. Stay out of the limelight, keep to the background, and you're never the primary target.

"Five?" Dad asks.

"At least," I say.

A quick succession of low-caliber shots echo through the cabin. It's got to be Roger using Dad's bedroom window as a vantage point.

Another maelstrom of bullets riddles the interior of the cabin and once again I find myself on the floor. My reflexes are better than I thought.

Dad scoops up the dead man's assault rifle and returns fire through the window. "Fuck!" He slides back down and Freddy pops up and squeezes off a few shots.

"Warren." Roger's voice elongates Dad's name dramatically.

"I know! I can see!"

What can he see?

I shuffle back over to the window and slink up the wall. Dad waves at me to stay low, but I need to know what they saw. He stares at me, his eyes trying to force me back down to the floor.

Several more gunshots from upstairs.

I have to know.

"Joy, stay down," Dad says.

"What's out there?"

"Get back down!"

"What did you see?"

"Joy! You listen to me! Do as I say! Get back down!"

It's then that I notice Freddy. He's sitting there, shaking, his eyes nearly bulging from their sockets. What the hell did they see?

I hear a whirring sound, like the weed whacker Dad used to edge the lawn with after mowing back at home. It revs up with a sputtering choke and the only thing I can picture is a savage-looking chainsaw spiraling toward some bare flat stomach, ready to chew right through the teenage flesh.

Thanks for the visuals, Mr. Hooper.

What's left of the shutters are dangling from one side, cascading across at a severe angle. There's no need to pull them apart anymore. I just need to lean my head out and look.

More gunfire drowns out the whirring sound and I pull myself back against the wall. Dad's grandpa chose his wood wisely. Thank God for that. Anything less dense and we'd all have been shredded apart by now.

"The bunker!" Freddy is nearly in tears. He's shaking the rifle, holding it by the barrel like a neck that he's strangling the life out of.

Dad looks over at him and yells over the gunfire, "Stay with me, Freddy!"

"The bunker!" he shouts again.

Dad's gaze turns to me and I can tell he knows it's our only hope. "Roger! Get down here!" he yells.

"What?" And I hear more Peacemaker shots from above.

"Cover me!" Dad says to Freddy, and tosses him the assault rifle. Freddy musters some sort of bravado, extends up and shoots out at our attackers.

Dad's shoving the couch across the floor, the stubby legs gouging into the wood. It's not going quick enough for him and he ends up grabbing it at its center base and flipping it onto its back so he can boot it out of his way.

The heavy area rug comes up easily, revealing what I've only seen a handful of times.

I look up when I hear the rumble of Roger barreling down the hallway, then the staircase. He lands expertly at the base and picks up Dad's discarded shotgun.

"Warren."

And Dad gathers a few shells from his pocket and tosses them to Roger. They're moving in sync, like some buddy cop duo from the 80s that somehow know what the other is thinking.

But it's not till Roger hears the beeping that he even notices what Dad's standing over. An electronic keypad.

The series of beeps continues as Dad inputs the code. A suctioning sound, like an airlock unlatching, and the floor eases open to reveal a hidden hatch beneath the wood planks. The hydraulics do most of the work, but Dad helps it along to hasten the process.

A bright light illuminates him from below, like an uncle holding a flashlight under his chin, telling ghost stories to his adolescent nieces and nephews.

Crawling across the floor, my hands and knees pressing down into an incalculable number of glass slivers, I make my way across the room toward the hatch.

Roger waits for me at the base of the stairs, loading rounds into the shotgun. He touches me between the shoulder blades, giving me a gentle push forward, silently assuring me he'd be in tow.

The bullets are still peppering in from outside. A horizontal waterfall of metal chipping away at the very structure of the cabin.

Roger and I reach the hatch, its top opening toward the front door like one of those ancient Roman shield walls. I hear Dad yell, "Freddy, come on!"

Oh God. He's still back there.

I see him, balled up beneath the windowsill, his eyelids pursed so tightly I'm afraid they'll squish his eyes into nothing.

"Freddy!" Dad screams again.

He doesn't move.

"Freddy! Please!" I yell. My voice cuts through the noise and our eyes lock. *Come on*, I mouth at him, and he nods, his bravery meter slowly filling back up. He slings the strap of the assault rifle over his chest and begins army crawling toward us.

"You're almost there," Roger says.

Dad's unarmed now, standing behind the hatch door, his legs straddling over the heavenly mouth of the sanctuary below. "Come on, Freddy," he cheers.

The encouragement has elated him, and I can almost make out a smile on his face. He scampers toward us, surely seeing the angelic glow emitting from the bunker.

Roger's hand extends, his fingers reaching for Freddy's—willing him to latch on so he can pull him in.

And the front door bursts open again. The man standing before us may as well have been a replica of the first. The same black tactical gear, a faceless entity, this one armed with a tactical shotgun, ready to fire.

It happens before Freddy can even turn his head. The close-quarter blast rips him in half at the waist and his body slams to the floor.

"Freddy!" I scream as Roger pulls me behind the hatch shield.

Another shot rings out, sparking off the lid. Dad shoves me down through the maw, my feet missing the metal rungs of the ladder, and I land hard against the grate below.

Another shotgun blast and Roger lands beside me. Was he hit?

The twang of shot ricocheting off metal.

Dad is on the ladder above us, both hands wrapped around the rubber-laden handle, pulling the hatch closed. The clattering of boots above, and the tactical shotgun fires one more blast down at us before the lid seals shut with a radiating hiss.

12

I've never seen it before. I knew it existed. Dad told me about it the first day we arrived. But he always said it was a last resort. He'd go down from time to time "to check on things" but I was never allowed to join him.

Well, here we are.

This place, with its sterile, unnaturally white glow... it doesn't get much more Kubrickian than this. Large lamplights lining the low ceiling. It's a corridor, extending out toward another mysterious doorway.

It's weird to say, but even in a moment like this, my mind goes back to cinema. All those films I've grown up on. The movies we watched over and over. God, I love them.

Must be a coping mechanism. I just saw a man cut in half by a shotgun, for Christ's sake.

Roger's still on his back, his fall having knocked the wind right out of him. His face and upper body are splattered with blood. I'm fairly certain none of it is his.

I can hear dull banging coming from the other side of the hatch. Hammering, or gunshots, I can't tell which. But Dad looks confident as he hops down from the ladder beside us and asks, "You alright?"

I do a quick self-inspection and nod. Dad nods back without another word and heads down the corridor. I help Roger to his feet and we follow. Dad's hand presses against a gel-filled pad. A light inside throbs, then we hear an off-tone beep and the door latch releases, inviting us inside.

As Roger and I soak in the surreal sight, Dad locks the door behind us, and that same odd beep echoes. Nearly everything is white, save for the modern-looking splashes of accent color here and there. A kitchen, living room, sleek dining table, and a few closed doors that I assume must be bedrooms and a bathroom. There's a glass wall showcasing a greenhouse full of fruits, vegetables, and herbs.

Dad goes to the monitors—two large screens suspended from the ceiling, displaying a dozen live camera feeds of both the interior and exterior of the cabin above us.

I see three of the intruders trying to break open the hatch with crowbars, but can't hear anything. The layers of metal and cement we've descended through easily block it all out.

"How secure is this place?" Roger asks.

"No way they're gettin' down here," Dad says.

We all keep watching the men on the monitors.

"You're sure?"

Dad is the first to notice the speckles of blood that have trailed behind me like breadcrumbs. He pulls a first-aid kit from the closet and crouches down beside me. I'd completely forgotten about the cut.

"I'm sure," he finally answers while cleaning and dressing my wound. The fact that I had a piece of someone's skull inside me seems so trivial after what happened to Freddy. So... insignificant.

Dad tucks the kit back into the closet, crosses to the kitchen, and pulls out a mason jar full of clear, syrupy liquid from the refrigerator. He twists off the lid and takes a drink. I can smell it immediately. Like gasoline and peaches. I've never seen Dad drink anything but tea and water. Whatever this is, it's neither.

His eyes settle on Roger, on Freddy's blood painted across his face and chest and sleeves. "There's a bathroom back there." And he points. "Shower off. I can't look at that."

Roger hesitates, glancing at the monitors, at the men milling about around the hatch. They haven't made any more progress. Then he turns to me, as if checking in for my approval. I'm not sure why, so I just nod at him.

"First door on the left is a bedroom. Grab some fresh clothes from the closet," Dad instructs him.

A moment passes, and it's just me and Dad, like it was at the start. Pipes rattle above us, but only for a minute, and Dad tells me it's just the boiler sending hot water to the bathroom. Hasn't been used in a bit.

I lean my .30-06 against the couch and settle down beside it. Dad already asked me once if I was alright. I don't expect him to do it again. Instead, we just occupy the space together in silence, both of us watching the screens like some messed-up family TV time.

The men are rummaging through everything. Pulling out drawers, flipping over furniture, searching closets. It's not until one of them lifts Freddy's corpse by the arm, revealing his shredded torso, that Dad tells me to stop watching. Before I look away completely, the man unzips his pants and pees on the side of Freddy's head.

My stomach turns, and I feel whatever's been dissolving in my stomach surge back up into my mouth. My cheeks are full with the sour taste, my hands clamped over my lips to keep from spewing it all out across the glowing floor. I make a move for the bathroom, forgetting Roger is showering, then quickly course-correct and throw my head into the kitchen sink and release.

Somehow that isn't all of it, and more vomit finds its way out of me, between my fingers, into the drain. Dad spins on the faucet and helps rinse my hands. I wipe my mouth, my chin, then rub an additional few handfuls over the rest of my face, as if I could somehow clean off my memory.

Dad walks me back to the couch and pivots the monitors away from view. Then he snags the mason jar off the coffee table and offers me a drink. I shake my head—if I had anything left to throw-up, the scent of the liquid would have made me puke again.

"It'll help."

"Help what?" I ask him.

"Your mind." Dad nudges the air in front of me with the base of the jar, gently sloshing the contents.

I try not to inhale as I bring it up to my lips. As soon as it hits my tongue, I feel a burn, like a whole layer is seared off, leaving it raw. Reminds me of how it feels after eating too many Sour Patch Kids. The peach flavor is strong, but not enough to cover up the other taste. I cough, and it makes the back of my throat burn. A warmth fills my body, and I pull my knees up to my chest.

Dad squeezes my shoulder and takes a drink for himself. Are we even tasting the same thing? He breathes in deep, as if consuming it were some kind of religious awakening. Whatever that religion is called, I won't be a participating member.

ROGER LOOKS LIKE A NEW MAN. Freshly cleaned and shaved. He's wearing clothes that were clearly meant for Dad, and they don't quite fit him right. The pants are a size or two too big and he has them cinched tight with his belt. The shirt—a long sleeve flannel—is tight around his arms and chest.

At least the blood is gone.

It's my turn to shower next, and it takes forever to get all the glass and wood splinters out of my hair. Even after I'm all dried off and in my new wardrobe, I still feel little fragments lingering, like the ghost sensation you get after pulling off a spiderweb you've walked through.

I reenter the living area as Roger tries to strike up a conversation with Dad. "This place is amazing." He's pulled down a book from the shelf, a pulpy looking paperback with a yellow raft flowing into the mouth of a giant skull on the cover. He flips through it, then slides the book back and gestures at the mason jar still in Dad's hand—only half of it remains. "You feel like sharing?"

Dad holds it out, and Roger graciously accepts. He cringes as soon as it hits his lips. Good. So I'm not the only one.

"Yikes. You make this yourself?" Roger hands it back and Dad takes a long swig.

"Yeah."

"I'm sorry about Freddy."

Dad doesn't look at him. "Yeah."

"I liked him. He was a good man."

Dad gives a slight chuckle and offers the mason jar to Roger again. He takes another sip, and this time his reaction is more reserved. His tongue's probably too numb now to taste anything.

"How much of this do you have stored down here?" Roger asks.

"Not nearly enough. Saved most of the room for food. Tried to stay level-headed when I prepped it all. I've got an off-grid wind generator out back. Couple solar panels on the roof. Got five different forms of power generation through the cabin, in fact. Gasoline in airtight containers buried out front. This place down here, like I said before, it's a last resort. Space is tight, no windows, no sunlight. Spend too much time in a place like this, it's bound to make anyone lose their wits. But here we are."

"Here we are," Roger repeats.

It's not until that moment that they notice I'm standing in the room with them. Roger greets me with as much of a smile as he can muster as I take a seat on the couch.

"What now?" I ask.

"We wait," Dad says. "I stocked the bunker so three people could survive for twelve months. At that point, we'd need to bring in more food."

"How long ago was this built?"

"Two years before the Shit. The cabin was my granddad's. Had it completely disassembled when I installed the bunker and then put back just the way it was afterward," Dad says, his words a bit slurred. "I visited and came down here periodically for upkeep and restock—to check on the plants and upgrade the clothes for Joy as she grew."

"Your construction business must have been booming," Roger says, taking another sip.

Dad clears his throat. "What?"

"Freddy told me you and him were construction contractors before the Shit. I'm saying business must have been good in order to afford to build all this."

Dad gives me a side eye. Roger's too focused on the mason jar to notice the exchange.

Good old Freddy. He may have had a big mouth, but at least he was smart enough to lie when it was necessary.

"You do what you have to do." Dad sits beside me on the couch and drapes his arm over my shoulders, pulling me in securely.

13

Dad suggests Roger and I look around and familiarize ourselves with the bunker. I know he wants to watch the monitors and doesn't have the energy to tell me I can't join him. I do my best not to argue with him, especially since the Shit. But I was my mother's daughter and debating was in my blood.

"Maybe I should stay and help—"

"Joy."

I take the hint, give him his space, and tell Roger to check out the greenhouse with me. It's bigger than it looked through the glass wall. Rows of plants, some of them growing in a hydroponic system, make it difficult to see the furthest end of the room. The grated floor is covered in a fine layer of dew that we stroll casually across as if we're at some garden store—pretending like life's normal again.

It feels nice.

Fake.

But nice.

"I saw you shoot one of them up there," I say, keeping my back to him as I walk ahead. "Guess that shows you don't have any issue killing soldiers."

"I take issue killing anyone," he replies. "But if I'm gonna do it, it'll be out of self-defense. Or to protect someone else."

"That what happened before? To make you run?"

"Awfully astute of you."

I can put two and two together, but it's nice to hear the compliment all the same. I keep my voice low. Dad will need to stay in the dark as long as possible. I'd say there's no telling what he would do, but that would be a lie. I know what he'd do. And so does Roger.

"Tell me what happened."

"I don't enjoy talking about it."

"You want me to trust you? I need to know the whole story."

He stops beside a cluster of mint and rubs a leaf between his thumb and index finger. "Joy, sometimes things just need to go unsaid."

I ignore him. "Where were you stationed?"

He looks over his shoulder, watching Dad through the glass wall. His attention is fully devoted to the monitors, and whatever he's seeing, it's not good. "You mean before we were called back to the States? Or after?"

"After."

"Pennsylvania border."

"What was your job?"

It looks like it's physically painful for him to answer. "To follow orders. I ended up not being very good at it after a while."

"After a while?"

"And you? Where were you and your dad?"

"Virginia."

I see his wheels turn. I shouldn't have said that. Should have lied, taken a hint from Freddy.

"That's really far east from here," he says.

"Tell me about it." I pluck a sprig of rosemary and smell it.

"Your Dad didn't have papers?"

"Not the right ones."

He nods.

"But a military ID will get you just about anywhere, right?"

"That's right. Until it's flagged," he says.

A mist hisses out of the ceiling, a timed burst, wetting the plants. It startles me and I instinctually reach for my rifle that isn't there. How embarrassing. You'd think I had PTSD from a snake attack or something. Roger didn't even react at all.

Cutting past the awkwardness I ask, "Was it really just a coincidence that you happened upon Freddy?"

Roger gives me one of those sad-type smiles. "Freddy was a good guy. I'm gonna miss him."

It wasn't an answer. And at the same time, it very much was. But before I can prod further...

"Roger," Dad calls. He's standing in the glass doorway. "I need you to come see something."

WE STAND THERE, side by side, staring up at the monitors.

"You ever seen one of those before today?" Dad asks.

Roger continues to watch the feed, his sense of security quickly vanishing. "No."

This must be what they all saw up there. The source of that chainsaw-ish sound. I understand now why they reacted the way they did. A bipedal machine, operated by one of the soldiers, stands atop the hatch, an arm-like extremity with a drill at the end, like some giant, spiraling metallic ice cream cone, sparks off the hatch lid, sending tiny, red hot fragments whipping in all directions.

"It can't penetrate the hatch... can it?"

Dad doesn't look so certain.

It begins to smoke, and the appendage raises away from the lid, the stubby hydraulic legs backing up. One soldier douses the drill with a bucket of water and a white cloud of steam sizzles into the air.

"Dad?"

"No. No, it can't get through. Even if it did, it can't fit down through the opening, and there's a whole other door to get past."

He looks at Roger, analyzing whether his answer was convincing. It wasn't.

14

———

This bed is a lot more comfortable than the one I had in the cabin. The sheets smell like lavender and the pillows are cool. I want to believe Dad when he told us the bunker was completely secure, but I keep my rifle with me all the same.

They must assume I'm asleep, that I can't hear them if they speak in whispers. But whatever's in that mason jar must have dulled their senses, because their voices are loud enough to make it through the closed door.

"They'll have to leave, eventually. Unless they go huntin', they'll run out of food," I hear Dad say.

"Did you grow up a hunter, Warren?"

"I spent all my summers in that cabin up there, from as early on as I can recall."

"Three generations out in the woods."

"Yeah."

A pause in the conversation. They must be passing a new jar back and forth.

"And then you taught Joy."

"She's been holdin' a gun since she was four years old. Killed everythin' from rabbits and squirrels to moose."

I've hated every minute spent hunting though.

"Which makes you proud, that she's carried on that old... family tradition."

I don't hear a response from Dad. I wonder if he's nodding.

"Do you think those hunting skills are the reason she's been able to make it this long?" Roger asks.

"It's helped. If anythin' happens to me, I know she'll be able to keep goin' because of what I've spent her whole life teachin' her."

My whole life? Summers, I guess. Sometimes during winter break. Saying he's taught me wilderness survival my whole life makes it sound like I was raised in the cabin.

I'm a city girl. How could I not be with mom's career? The cabin was a vacation spot. One of many, actually. I never liked hunting with Dad, but he insisted I learn. Because he knew. Somehow, he knew it would all end up like this.

I wonder if Mom knew too. If she did, she never said so. Her job was stressful. I would've had to be completely out of it not to see that. But she loved it. I'm not really sure which parts of it, but there was something she liked. The attention? She almost had celebrity status. The influence? That couldn't be denied.

Power? I'd heard other people say it. Heard them vilify her and what she stood for. I didn't give a crap about any of that, though. The last thing I wanted to do was follow in her line of work. She had her interests, and I had mine. But one thing we saw eye to eye on?

Movies.

If I had one single wish—of course, it'd be Mom.

But I also really wanted my movies back.

Grandpa must not have been a fan of films. There wasn't even a TV in the cabin. I wasn't expecting streaming service, but I would've settled for a DVD player. Or VHS. Yeah, I know what that is. Mom and I used to do "Saturday Night Oldies" on the box television we had with the built-in VHS player. All screened in low-def 4:3 aspect ratio.

It was our thing. The time we would snuggle up together and forget about everything else. Forget about school. Forget about her job. Forget about the world.

"And how 'bout you," Dad asks Roger. "You ever do any huntin'?"

"No. I don't think I could ever kill an animal unless it was for survival. Plenty of supermarkets where I grew up."

Listening to the growing camaraderie makes me smile. Must be that drink doing the talking, because I've never heard Dad converse so much, especially not with someone he's only recently met.

"Then how is it you're so familiar with firearms?" Dad asks, the casualness evaporating from his tone.

Shit.

There's a long pause. Should I get up? Should I go out there?

"How do you mean?" Roger finally replies.

"Well, there was the pistol you took off that Lawman Freddy killed, the one you first showed up here with. Then the Peacemaker. And my shotgun. Pretty wide range of familiarity."

I sit up in bed, leaning forward over the edge toward the door. What's Dad getting at?

Don't be stupid. You know what he's getting at. You know exactly what he's doing.

"You gotta pick up a few tricks to make it these days, right?" Roger responds.

Which one of them is holding that mason jar? Which one is sitting there, punctuating their sentences by taking a sip of it?

Dad says, "Freddy said you just happened upon him. Right place, right time sort of thing. That true?"

"Yeah. Lucky for us both, you could say."

My toes lower to the tile floor.

Dad chuckles. "Come on, now. Be honest with me. Yeah? If we're gonna be stuck down here together, may as well speak the truth."

I lift myself slowly, trying not to make a sound. The mattress is firm enough for me to slide off silently. I suppose no one's ever used it.

"I don't know what you want me to say, Warren."

"Freddy was out visiting the whorehouses."

"I gathered."

"I think maybe you saw him there. Figured he might be someone you could prey on."

"Prey on?" Roger's voice is indignant.

My jaw is clenched, hoping the floor won't creak as I move across it toward the door. I immediately feel foolish for thinking it, though. We're not in the cabin anymore. These aren't old wooden planks that I'm walking on. It's cold, white tile.

"Were you staying there? At one of the whorehouses? The Lawmen don't pry too much, from what Freddy tells me. They're almost a type of sanctuary."

I can't help but think of the Hunchback. Even standing there in front of the closed door, Dad and Roger's conversation slowly escalating, my head fills with images of the mysterious bell-ringer. Mom preferred the Maureen O'Hara film, but this was one time I had to disagree. That entire opening sequence in the animated version was—

"I'd prefer to think about the future. Focus on where we are going. How we'll—"

Dad cuts Roger off and says, "You saw him at the brothel, marked him as a man with something to offer, then followed him, waiting for an opportunity to persuade him into helping you."

I ease the handle down and crack the door open half an inch, just enough to see out into the living room area. Dad's sitting on the far end of the L-shaped couch, nearest the kitchen. Roger lounges at the opposite end, his back to me, hand cradling the empty mason jar on the arm of the sofa.

Roger scoffs. "Alright. Yeah. I saw him there. And I could tell he had a haven. Men who do, carry themselves differently. Just a tad bit more confidence in their demeanor."

Dad laughs. Not a chuckle. Not a snicker. It's an honest to God laugh. He slaps both palms down on his thighs and pulls himself up off the couch. Pointing at Roger, a slur in his voice, he says, "That's empty."

I can't see Roger's face, but I swear the tension in his shoulders eases with Dad's statement. He tilts the mason jar and says, "Yes, sir. It is."

Dad's already got his hand inside the refrigerator, pulling out another full vessel. He cranks the lid loose and sets it on the granite counter. "Confidence." And his head bobs rhythmically. "I don't know if that's a word anyone ever attributed to Freddy before."

He walks over to Roger and pours half the fresh liquid into his dry mason jar. "Thanks."

Dad settles back down on the other side and takes a sip. "My wife made this, you know."

I cringe at the thought. Mom made that? It's disgusting.

"It's good," Roger says.

"You can taste the peach, right?"

And Roger nods.

"She wasn't into roughin' it. Didn't care for campin', really. But she did it anyway. Did it because she knew it meant something to me. And the more she invested herself in the things I loved, the things that made me... me, she started findin' ways to make her own imprint. She didn't drink much. Well, in our younger years, yeah. We did plenty of drinkin'. Spent plenty of money on it. But after Joy was born, she pretty much stopped. Can't drink like that when you're pregnant, and afterward, well, she just never really started up again." Dad nods as if he's giving a stamp of approval.

He takes another drink and his gaze foggily drifts toward my door. Toward me. But somehow he doesn't notice I'm peering out at him through the crack.

"Me, on the other hand, I kept on drinking. I didn't think it was out of control or anything like that, not until she told me. Not until the time I almost..."

I've never heard him talk about anything like this. Almost what? What did he almost do?

"And then I stopped. Started with me not cracking open a beer as soon as I walked in the door. Then moved to not drinking until we put Joy to bed. And eventually," Dad shrugs. "I quit altogether."

Dad's eyes are wet, but he doesn't bother wiping them. I wish I could see Roger's face. How's he reacting to this—the recipient of my father's confession?

"Christ. Forgot how emotional this shit can make you. Sorry about that."

Roger adjusts the half-full mason jar in his hand, weighing its contents. "If there was ever a time to imbibe, this might be it, Warren."

Dad smirks, nods, and raises his jar to Roger, who returns the gesture, and they both drink. He lets out a satisfied sigh and says, "What was I saying?"

Good. The less Dad digs into Roger's past, the better for all of us.

Dad grins. "Freddy, yeah?"

Damn it.

"You followed him. Saved him. And in return, he brought you here. I got all that. But there's one thing I can't figure out."

Roger's fingers tighten as Dad continues.

"Freddy said that when you first pulled over, while he was getting his ass beat, you showed the Lawman your papers. And he just... let you go."

Go back to talking about your drinking. Please.

"So, that means you either had a really good fuckin' forgery, or those papers were legitimate. And if they were legitimate, it would mean that you're either registered with the people now in control of this country, or..."

And we both wait. Roger and I. Both knowing the next words that will breach Dad's lips. The hidden truth. The puzzle Dad's already put together.

"... you're military."

Shit. Shit. Shit.

And Roger drinks. And Dad drinks. Roger says, "Warren—"

Dad's off the couch, coming for him. Roger flings the mason jar, missing Dad's head by millimeters, shattering it against the wall.

Dad's fist finds Roger's face. Roger stumbles back into the bookshelf, knocking piles onto the floor around his feet. Dad grabs the muzzle of the assault rifle and he swings it at Roger, who leans back just in time to avoid the blow.

Roger throws a punch at Dad, who raises the rifle horizontally like a shield, causing Roger's fist to smack off the metal. He winces, then Dad slams the center of the gun into Roger's face, breaking his nose.

Blood spurts out across the floor. Dad brings the rifle in like a baseball bat, and Roger uses his forearm to protect himself, then retaliates immediately with two punches—one to Dad's gut, the other to his jaw.

Dad's knee finds Roger's groin and Roger hunches over in silent agony. I know it's a dirty move when I see it.

"No!" I shout as Dad brings the butt of the rifle slamming down on the back of Roger's head. I hear a crack and Roger drops to his knees. Then Dad's knee connects with Roger's blood-soaked face, knocking him flat on his back.

Dad stands over him, pointing the barrel down at his chest, and Roger stares up defiantly, blood pouring from his nose.

"Dad, don't!" I scream.

Roger's heel finds Dad's ankle and sends him to the floor. He rolls over on top of him, struggling to wrench the rifle from his grip. But as soon as he gains control of the weapon, Dad smacks it from his hands, sending it clattering out of reach across the floor.

Roger's hands constrict around Dad's neck, and Dad fights back wildly, trying to pry his throat free.

"Let him go!"

Roger's grip is tight, and Dad's strength is fading, his face red, eyes bulging.

I need my rifle. I need my rifle. I need my rifle.

When Roger hears the bolt-action, he freezes. Without loosening his fingers from Dad's neck, he slowly turns to me, seeing my .30-06, and my eye staring down the sights. My finger wraps lightly around the trigger.

"Put it down," Roger tells me.

My breathing is fast. Uneven. My hands trembling.

The life begins to fade from Dad's face, his eyes rolling backward. One hand is clenched around Roger's wrist, the other wildly attempting to grab hold of something, anything to use as a weapon.

"Put down the rifle, Joy."

Can I do this?

I will if he makes me. I'll kill him. Put a bullet right in his—

Then Roger stands and approaches me—releasing Dad, who gasps for air, filling his burning lungs. I take a step back and he rips the rifle from my hands, saying, "I wasn't going to—"

But he's not expecting me to have the steel pipe. I do it quick, pulling it from my waistband behind my back, bringing it savagely across the side of his head.

15

Dad's back in front of the monitors, holding an ice pack to his head. The soldiers upstairs in the cabin are still tearing our home apart. Searching.

Roger groans, slowly regaining consciousness. I wonder what he was dreaming about while he was out. Do you dream when someone bludgeons you with a metal pipe?

He sits on the floor, his hands tied above his head, secured to the bookshelf. His shirt is off, all his bruises visible. And, of course, his tattoo.

This is my fault. I should have told Dad when I first saw it. Christ, he almost killed my father. He almost ruined everything. All because I wanted to trust him. So stupid. I'm so stupid.

His eyes flutter open and the residual pain immediately reintroduces itself. Somehow Dad can tell he's awake again without bothering to take his gaze off the screens, and says, "You're one of them. All your lies. All your... And you're just one of them."

My fingers trace the grooves of my rifle as it rests in my lap.

"You ain't a scout. Not after the hell you gave them up there. So that means what? You're a deserter? Is that the reason they're here? 'Cause they tracked you down? Followed you to take you out?"

Roger tries to adjust his pose, but the cords are tight. "I don't think I'd be worth the trouble."

"No one's worth this much trouble."

"You two are."

I look at Dad, who's turned to face Roger for the first time.

"How's that?" he asks.

Roger scoffs. "Come on, Warren. You know why they want you. Joy told me you're from Virginia."

"And?"

"So I'm assuming you were a politician. Someone important. And that's why they've come."

"I wasn't a politician." Dad's eyes shift to me and as tears begin to form, he looks away. "But my wife was." The mixture of anger and anguish is almost leaking from his pores as he tries to remain stoic.

"Your wife?"

"She was a congressional representative. Tough as they come." He smiles genuinely at me as he says it. "And she was an exceptional mother."

The past tense is enough to tell Roger all he needs to know. But Dad continues on, as if it's some cathartic release.

"They built a gallows. Right there in front of everyone. Marched her and all the others up the steps, one after the other. Broadcasted live for the entire world to see. There I was, watchin' from our livin' room, unable to do a damn thing. I saw them... hang my wife. And I saw our military standby and let it happen."

Roger doesn't know what to say. The grieving shell that is my father recanting his horror tale, sharing what I can only imagine is so sadly similar to many others.

At what point did I start crying? I wipe my face dry and cross to the kitchen, starting some tea as a distraction.

"I let you in because that man up there vouched for you. But now—" Dad stops as something on the screen catches his eye. "Damn," he says, just above a whisper. It's not until I turn and see the monitors that I realize what he's reacting to.

In one of the feeds, a soldier reaches up with a gloved hand. Black covers the lens, and then it cuts out completely. They're discovering the surveillance cameras. Eight of the twelve video feeds have been disconnected, leaving four live rectangles spread across the two monitors.

"How did they find them? We've been here for sixteen months and I never even saw one."

"It's alright. There's still a few they haven't—"

The lights cut out, and we lose the entire bunker in darkness.

No-no-no-no.

A silent moment.

A hum. And then...

Green light fills the bunker.

"Backup power," Dad says. "Looks like they found the primary source." Roger and I exchange looks. "We'll be fine as long as they don't—"

A loud thud. We haven't been able to hear anything from up there. Not with as far down as we came. Not with how thick the bunker walls are. Whatever that was, it must have sounded like an explosion up above.

The ducts rattle violently, then go quiet.

Dad smiles in disbelief.

"Yeah," he laughs. "Alright."

What the hell is happening?

He walks over to the couch and slumps down into the cushions. Tossing the icepack beside him, he lets out an obnoxiously long sigh.

"What was that?" Roger asks.

"That? That was our air intake vents being blocked."

"What?"

"The air intake vents. There's four of them hidden around the exterior of the cabin. All setup with NBC filters. If they found them and blocked them up, we can't get breathable air down here."

"Then we bypass the vents," I say.

Dad ignores me. "These boys sure know what they're doin'."

"They're a flush team," Roger says. "It's what they've been trained for."

"Hey!" I shout, and Dad turns to me. "How do we bypass the intake vents?"

He thinks for a moment, Roger and I waiting with anticipation.

"Alright—the uh, the air duct runs the length of the cabin. It's below concrete, so we can't just punch up into the living room. But if we went out past the cabin, the concrete ends before the duct does, so we could potentially cut a hole in the duct to let the oxygen in. It's gotta be a fresh hole though, since they already found the original intake points."

I nod. That sounds like a solution.

Roger tries again to adjust into a less painful position on the floor. "As long as they don't hear us cutting or see us break through, then as far as they know, we'll suffocate down here. Maybe they'll move on at that point."

The water is boiling. As I fill Dad's cup, the sickly green light makes the process look surreal. Like some artsy sci-fi flick filled with alien brews and loose-leaf extraterrestrial clippings.

"It'll have to be you, Joy." I turn to him, the steam from the tea billowing up in front of my face, distorting his image. "You're the only one who can fit in the vent."

16

———————

My fingers slide between the fins and I lift the ceiling vent cover, tilting it to bring it down into the greenhouse. Handing it to Dad, I take another step up the ladder and poke my head into the duct. I can only see a few feet in either direction before the lime-colored light raising from the greenhouse drops off.

Crouching back down, perched a foot above Dad's head, I ask him, "Which way?" He points to his right and hands me a rubber-coated flashlight. "How will I know when I've passed the concrete?"

"It's about a hundred and fifty feet. I think you'll just have to give it your best guess."

"Alright."

"Stay quiet once you're in there. Remember, you only need to make a small hole. Four by four should do it." And he hands me a sheathed knife.

I look over at the glass wall. Roger is watching us from the other room, his arms still secured above his head to the bookshelf. "Be careful," I tell Dad.

He glances over his shoulder at Roger. "You just worry about the task at hand."

"Right." I tuck the knife into my belt, place the flashlight between my teeth and stand back up.

"Joy." Dad's staring up at me. "I love you."

It hits hard. I can't even remember the last time I heard him say those words. Before Mom, I guess.

Don't cry. Don't cry. Don't cry.

I click the torch on, and through the barricade between my teeth I mumble back, "Ruv you oo."

Lifting myself all the way up into the duct, I stretch out flat onto my stomach. It's not until I'm fully inside that I realize just how tight it really is. I thought I'd be able to army crawl my way with relative ease, but there's barely more than an inch on either side of my shoulders. I can't even lift my head up all the way before it hits the ceiling, and I'm forced to look up through my brow the way all the crazy characters do in Kubrick movies. Like Jack, and Alex and Private Pyle.

Inch by inch, I struggle forward at a gradual upward angle, my elbows basically glued to my sides, bumping against the walls with every push. My thighs and knees have even less luck. It's my boots though, that seem to hold me back the most, their rubber grip jerking against the floor like brake pads pressing down.

A hundred and fifty feet of this?

The angle at which I'm forced to hold my head makes it impossible to point the flashlight straight ahead. Instead, it sags, shooting its beam down only about two feet in front of my face. The light reflects into my eyes, blinding me, doing the exact opposite of what I need it to do.

I strain my neck to lift it higher, the top of my head brushing against the dusty metal as I wiggle my way onward. I can already feel the tension burning in my shoulder muscles and in my neck at the base of my skull.

My head dips only slightly, but it's enough to let the end of the flashlight hit the floor of the duct, the rubber halting it immediately. The shaft grates against my teeth and I swear I can feel one of them loosen.

God damnit!

Taking a deep breath to calm myself, I jut out my lower jaw like a trout and angle the flashlight back up.

Just. Keep. Going.

How far have I gone now? I instinctually try to look back over my shoulder to where I started, forgetting that the duct is far too constricting to allow me to turn.

Well, I haven't passed it, that's for sure.

The material of my clothes suddenly becomes very apparent to me as I move up the shaft. A loud, echoing, brushing sound. A street-sweeper clearing debris with coarse bristles. Surely it only sounds like this in here, right?

I let the sound become a metronome, keeping me calm and focused as I continue towards my target. I count the sections of the duct as I pass by to gauge my distance. Should have done this from the start. Fifteen or so more and I'll give it a shot.

Then something grabs hold of my waist and I can't move any further. What the hell? Again I try to turn, but it's too tight. I attempt to pull forward, but whatever it is has snagged hold of one of my belt loops on the right side. Pressing my left elbow into the floor, raising my stomach just enough for my right arm to coil underneath and reach for my belt, I try to slide my hand back to fish it free. I feel along the leather, the first belt loop to the right of the buckle, then the next one over. Both seem to be unrestrained. From the angle I'm at, the third loop is just out of reach. Located just behind my hip, my fingers fondle for it blindly.

Come on. Come on.

I grab hold of my waistband and pull inward, trying to twist my pants enough to reach the third belt loop—but whatever has snared it won't let it move an inch. I tug harder. Still no luck.

Maybe if I adjust a little this way.

Or like this?

A surge of heat radiates through my body as the notion that I'm trapped sets in. This is how mice feel. Their little toes stuck to the glue, unable to pull themselves free, waiting for something bigger to arrive and crush them.

My shoulders clunk against the walls as I squirm. Is the duct getting smaller? No. That's ridiculous. Just calm down.

But my metronome is gone—stunted by whatever has its claws around my belt loop. My boots press down, their rubber gripping, and the floor of the duct thuds dully as I try to leverage my hips enough to wrestle to loop free. The flashlight sags again and my teeth almost drop it, my jaw aching.

This isn't working. God. It won't come loose.

My body thrashes almost involuntarily. Like a dog trying to jerk itself free from its collar, I flail about in a sudden bout of panic. The duct sways, the pounding echoing in a crescendo of noise.

Then I stop, and my whole body seizes up as I force myself to freeze. Stop it! They're going to hear you.

Take a breath—

I already tried that. It won't come loose.

It's just a belt loop.

I can't get myself free.

It's just hooked on something. Maybe a screw or a small bit of metal from the duct wall. Just back up.

I tried backing up.

Did you?

Of course I did. I'm not stupid.

Then why are you making so much noise? Sounds like a pretty stupid thing to do in this circumstance.

I know! I know!

Just back up.

Okay. Alright. But I'm telling you, I already—

And with just an ounce of pressure, somehow whatever was holding me back, let's go. And I'm free.

I close my eyes and rest my head against the cool metal for a moment, letting my pulse lower.

Alright. I nod to myself. Alright.

I resume inching my way down the duct, led by the tilted beam. I count the sections as I go, and when I pass the fifteenth one since I began counting, I stop.

Here. This is where I'll do it.

It takes every bit of mental strength I have to remain serene as I shuffle onto my shoulder, then onto my back, so that I'm facing up at the ceiling. The flashlight's beam is once again bouncing right back in my face, reflecting off the metal ceiling only inches from my nose. I let it drop out of my mouth. Don't need it anymore.

My fingers find my belt, then the rigid grip of the knife, and delicately slide it from its sheath. I move slowly, not wanting to accidentally bang the blade on something and knock it out of my hands. Then I realize—

This isn't going to work.

The knife is too long. The space between my body and the ceiling, too short. There's no way for me to get it pointed upright to stab through the duct. And even if I rolled onto my shoulder and gained a few more inches of space for the blade to go vertical beside me, I don't have enough room to jab it up with enough force to break through the metal.

Panic sets in again.

I have to go back and tell Dad.

Stop it!

I have to. This won't work.

Stop and think.

I am thinking.

You're not. You're reacting.

There's not enough room in here to do this.

Then you're going to die.

What?

Then you're going to die. If you can't stop and figure something out here, you're going to die. And so is Dad. And so is Roger. Because you won't just stop and think for a minute.

I *can* stop and think.

Then do it.

I pause a moment, my mind settling down. I press the edge of the blade against the metal ceiling and begin rubbing it back and forth like a saw along a four or five-inch area. Little metal spirals snake off and land on my face like popping embers. Over and over, I rock the blade until it finally perforates the ceiling. I move the knife over four inches and start on a parallel cut. It's not long before I have three sides of a square sliced into the metal above my chin.

I insert the tip of the blade and pull the metal tongue down, then carefully spin the knife in my hand and use the butt of the grip to bend and fold it backward. Laying the knife across my chest, I feel around beside my head for the flashlight. Clicking it on, I can see a solid wall of dirt levitating beyond the hole in the metal. My fingers slide up into the stony soil, easily piercing through the first inch, which tumbles down onto my face.

I turn away, the debris scattering into my eyes and nostrils, sticking to my lips. Then, almost immediately, my fingers feel the resistance as the dirt becomes more densely compacted. The space beneath my finger nails fills as I scrape and claw through the small opening. Taking the knife again, I stab up at the dirt from an awkward angle, each hit sprinkling more and more soil across me. Then the earth gives and a rush of dirt cascades down into the duct, piling up over my chest and neck and face. For a moment I don't think it's ever going to stop and I imagine myself buried alive in the tiny shaft.

I shuffle a foot further up the vent to get my head clear, coughing out sticky saliva-mixed with debris that comes out as pasty globs. I try to stifle the noise as I clear my nose and throat to avoid choking.

When the dirt flow stops, I brush some of it aside and reach my arm up through the square, my sleeve snagging and shredding open on the jagged edges. More of the soil tumbles down around my arm as it extends further and I raise my chest to the ceiling of the duct to stretch as far as I can. My fingers wiggle, feeling for some sign that I've breached the surface. The breeze feels chilly as it blows across my skin.

I did it.

I did it!

I pull my arm back into the duct and shimmy down so that my face is directly below the square. The evening redness in the sky is all I can see. It's all I needed to see. A smile widens across my face as I gaze up at my success.

I did it.

The whirring of a drill revving up instantly makes my entire body feel numb. Monstrous footsteps rattle the duct and something leans over the hole I've created, blotting out the sunset.

<h1 style="text-align:center">17</h1>

The spinning metal pierces down at my face, tearing effortlessly through the duct. I scoot down to get out of range, but the drill snags a handful of my hair, twisting it up around its cone shape, ripping a patch of flesh from my scalp.

I can't help but scream. There's no point staying quiet anymore. They know I'm here.

Dirt flies in all directions as the drill retracts back through the massive hole it created. I'm still shuffling back toward Dad when it chews its way down at me again, this time spiraling between my calves, slicing a chunk out of my left leg.

I feel hands scoop under my arms and I'm dragged up into the waning light through the first hole. Before I even have eyes on my attacker, I'm stabbing.

My knife hits the protective shielding of a tactical vest with my first strike, but my second finds meat. Before the man can react, I sink the blade into his armpit two more times. His grip releases and I fall to the ground.

The soldier operating the walking drill takes a step toward me, revving the twirling apparatus. I already have the dead man's rifle in my hands and I fire off a burst of gunfire at the machine's windshield. The bullets crack the first layer of glass, but cannot break through.

That thing may be powerful, but it's slow. I step around to the windowless door and execute the operator. His head opens up like a pistachio shell. Seeing the gore so close sends a surge of nausea coursing through my stomach and I dry heave.

I can hear someone running up behind me, but I turn too late. His gloved hand wrenches the barrel of the machine gun out of my grasp and his other fist finds my jaw. I hear the crack, like someone breaking a whole boxful of spaghetti in half. The pain splinters out in all directions, swelling around every inch of my head.

I'm back on the ground and the man is on top of me, pinning my arms, straddling over my waist. I buck my legs and bring my knees into his back, but it doesn't phase him.

Another soldier stands above us, pulling his balaclava down around his neck, revealing his sweat-covered face. "Fucking bitch," he calls me. He bends down next to my head and backhands me across my shattered jaw. I feel the broken pieces jostle about beneath my skin, like discarded scraps in a garbage bag. I try to stare him down, focus my eyes on his in a display of defiance, but the pain is too great. Tears fill my eyes and I squeeze them tight.

And as the pain escalates, my mind unplugs.

18

I find myself inside the cabin again, sitting on the back of the overturned couch. They're holding me up by the shoulders, balancing me, tilting my broken chin up to face one of the last remaining security cameras that I'm seeing for the first time. It's camouflaged so well amongst the knots in the wood paneling.

How did they see it?

I try to jerk free and feel the burn of cord around my wrists, securing them behind my back. My knees are tied together as well, making it impossible for me to run if I wanted to. The men on either side of me are pointing up at the camera, then pointing at me, shouting obscenities through their masks.

They're threatening to hurt me. To kill me. Unless Dad and Roger come out of the bunker and give themselves up. I didn't hear any audio feed on the monitors when I was down there, but if Dad's watching, I know he can surmise what they're getting at.

Don't come out! I want to scream it at the top of my lungs. But my jaw won't move. And that's when the pain kicks in again.

They'll only kill you too!

You know they will!

They'll kill all of us if you leave the bunker.

Even if I could say it, and even if Dad could hear it, I know he wouldn't listen. What kind of parent could leave their daughter to the mercy of people like this?

I was his weakness. Maybe if I hadn't coughed inside the duct they wouldn't have found me. I screwed it all up. I got us all killed.

A few more minutes of the men shouting at the camera and then they drag me out the front door. The heels of my boots carve trenches through the dirt as they pull me along, out toward the tree line.

I can feel my face swelling into some deformed shape. If I had a mirror, I wouldn't be surprised to see Quasimodo looking back at me. God, I miss my films. I miss Mom. I miss so many things.

They lift me up and stand me inside Dad's wheelbarrow beneath the limb of a tree. One soldier keeps hold of me by my belt, while another stands with his back to me, wrestling with a substantial amount of black parachute cord.

The front door of the cabin is open, and from where they have me, I can see straight into the living room. What I assume are the remaining three soldiers, are standing guard beside the sealed hatch, waiting for Dad to give into their demands.

He's coming out here. Not to save me, because we both know he can't. He's coming out to show me he loves me. That he'd do anything for me. Give everything.

Please don't.

He has to.

No, he doesn't. He can just stay in there. We don't all have to die.

He can't do that, Joy.

Yes, he can! Tell him not to be stupid!

Dad's voice is an echo in my memory. "I'm here for you, baby. We're here for each other. No matter what happens."

And the hatch lid opens.

The soldiers' guns ever ready—Dad and Roger emerge from the glow below, their empty hands raised in the air. They march them out through the front door and Dad screams at the sight of me standing in the wheelbarrow.

I can't hear what he's saying. I just see the anger exploding from his face, his mouth open, roaring like a wild animal. One of the soldiers slams the butt of their machine gun into his nose and he drops to his knees, blood pouring out onto the soil.

Roger just stares at me with an expression of helplessness. Something about that makes me feel better. A mutual understanding that this is the end and there's nothing any of us can do.

Dad, cradling his slathered face, looks up at me as they loop the noose around my neck. I try to smile at him, but I'm not sure if he can tell.

A soldier crouches down in front of him, shouting, pointing at me. He's probably saying something like, "This is what you get. This is what happens when you don't think the way we think."

Why can't I hear anything?

Maybe my body's already shutting down.

Maybe my brain just can't handle any more.

Whatever the reason, it's a blessing.

They shove Roger to his knees and without so much as a final word, they put a bullet in the back of his head. It all happens so quickly, I don't even have time to look away.

And Dad's still screaming, reaching for me. His fingers claw at the air between us. The soldier continues to point at me.

I wish I could tell Dad it will all be okay. That's what they do in the movies. I want to jump down and run into his arms and comfort him. I'd hold him tighter than ever, squeeze him so hard that he'd wince. I hope he knows that's what I want to do.

I try to think about something else. Mom. Snuggling together on the couch, watching one of our favorites. Back when we would forget about school. Forget about work. Forget about the world.

AFTERWORD

This story has had quite the journey. I originally wrote *Woodhaven* as a screenplay. It placed in several competitions, including the 2016 Austin Film Festival Screenplay Competition, 2016 PAGE International Screenwriting Awards, and the 2016 Final Draft Big Break Screenplay contest. For a short period between 2017 and 2018, it looked like it was going to get optioned by a production company that had an interest in bringing it to the big screen, but unfortunately, that never came to fruition.

However, I was told that during that time, Christoph Waltz had read the script, loved it, and was considering coming onboard the project to play Warren if it got off the ground. I never spoke to him personally, but the thought of one of my all-time favorite actors even reading something I'd written, much less enjoying it, was an indescribable feeling.

For a few years I set the script aside, overall bummed-out that I'd put so much time and effort into something that ended up amounting to basically my first step into the world of Hollywood, and simultaneously my first time having my nose broken by the door slamming back in my face.

After writing my first novel, *Beasts of the Caliber Lodge*, I began working on several follow-ups, but in August 2021, I read Max Booth III's *We Need To Do Something*, and the single location/small cast setup immediately made me think about *Woodhaven* again, which shares a similar minimalist dynamic. The next day I pulled out that original screenplay I'd written that got me into those competitions, and I began translating it into prose form. This book, as you've just read it, is very close to the original screenplay, with only a few changes.

While the movie version has yet to happen, it feels amazing to put this story out in the world, available for people to see what almost became a major motion picture back in 2018.

Thank you, dear reader, for taking the time to visit the cabin and let Joy tell you her story.

-L.J. Dougherty

ABOUT THE AUTHOR

L.J. Dougherty is the author of the Espionage Horror novels, *Beasts of the Caliber Lodge*, and *Primal Reserve*, which he published in January 2021 and January 2022, respectively. *Woodhaven* is his third book. He lives in California with his amazing wife, talented son, and goofy dog.

You can find L.J. on social media.

On Twitter @LJ_Dougherty
    On Instagram @l.j.dougherty

Or via email at LJDoughertyAuthor@gmail.com

ACKNOWLEDGMENTS

<u>VERY SPECIAL THANKS</u>

To my wife and partner in crime, Tia, who supports my creativity while "Life, uh... finds a way." Thank you for reading all those dozens of screenplay drafts and providing feedback back when I first wrote this story.

To my son Declan, who balances all the darkness in this world with his infectious smile and endless humor.

To my pals, Cameron & Tim, for reading every single thing I've written for the past 19ish years before anyone else lays eyes on it, and for providing feedback and edit suggestions.

ALSO BY

L.J. Dougherty

BEASTS OF THE CALIBER LODGE

A Novel of Espionage Horror

1965.

Jimmy Knotts has grown accustomed to the danger involved with his line of work. Hunting escaped Nazis across multiple continents has whittled him down to a focused predator. When his latest lead brings him to an elite hunting lodge in the Alaskan frontier, Jimmy is ushered into a frozen realm of territorial monsters unlike any he's ever encountered.

Pulp horror meets international intrigue in an adventure full of icy suspense, **cinematic ultra-violence... and Sasquatches.**

"If Spielberg made a Bigfoot movie, it would be like *Beasts of the Caliber Lodge.* L.J. Dougherty perfectly blends the old school charm of a 60s spy thriller with wild horror and mayhem to make a unique Bigfoot story that really stands out among the rest."

—Cameron Roubique, author of *Kill River*

BEASTS
of the
CALIBER LODGE
L.J. Dougherty

ALSO BY

L.J. Dougherty

PRIMAL RESERVE
A Novel of Espionage Horror

Set in the world of **Espionage Horror**, *Primal Reserve* is the pulpy, **blood-soaked** follow-up to *Beasts of the Caliber Lodge.*

"Original, thrilling and utterly gripping — *Primal Reserve* has more twists and turns than the Amazon River, which kept me on tenterhooks as the action, horror and story unfolded around me. Buy the book, take the ride, you will not be disappointed."

—Ross Jeffery, Bram Stoker Award nominated author of *Tome*

"Dougherty has done it again. *Primal Reserve* is a thrilling trip into the heart of darkness, a violent espionage horror, custom-built to excite and unsettle."

—David Sodergren, author of *The Forgotten Island*

"*Primal Reserve* is a stay-up-all-night triumph of a novel, a thrilling tale conveyed in lyrical, addictive prose that calls for nothing less than binge-reading. You're going to have a lot of fun with this one. Highly recommended!"

—Brian Bowyer, author of *Flesh Rehearsal*

PRIMAL
RESERVE
L.J. Dougherty